Running on Empty in the Fast Lane

REDEFINING SUCCESS

Curt Dodd

ACCENT BOOKS
Denver, Colorado

Unless otherwise noted, all Scripture references are taken from the *New International Version* of the Bible © 1978 by New York International Bible Society, published by the Zondervan Corporation. Used by permission.

Several illustrations adapted from the *Encyclopedia of 7,700 Illustrations: Signs of the Times* by Paul Lee Jan, ThD., Assurance Publishers. Used with permission.

A division of Accent Publications, Inc.
12100 West Sixth Avenue
P.O. Box 15337, Denver
Colorado 80215

Copyright © 1990 Accent Publications, Inc.
Printed in the United States of America

All rights reserved. No portion of this book may be reproduced in any form without the written permission of the publishers, with the exception of brief excerpts in magazine reviews.

Library of Congress Catalog Card Number 89-63650

ISBN 0-89636-260-4

To Cleo Blake Dodd,
My Mother

*Her example and encouragement
has taught me to never stop
striving,
reaching,
dreaming.*

ACKNOWLEDGMENTS

Success in anyone's life is never an isolated, independent experience. Besides the obvious touch of God's hand, special people must share the credit. The successful completion of this project is no less the same.

Deserving the lion's share is Mary Nelson, my editor at Accent. It was her personal belief in this book that made it a reality. Subsequently, she shared in the formulation and expression of many of the chapters. I am indeed indebted to her for her selfless efforts to see this work through to its final stage.

Quietly, behind the scenes, Gina Leonard, my secretary has researched, edited, and typed. Her integral role has been the organizational adhesive for the manuscript.

These two godly women share in the victory of this book.

Dr. Curt Dodd

Contents

	Introduction	7
1/	The Winner's Edge	9
2/	Positive Perspectives	12
3/	Perplexing Situations	21
4/	Persistent Priorities	27
5/	Personal Purity	39
6/	Internal Incentives	48
7/	It's Who You Know	58
8/	Failure Pays	66
9/	Powerful Principles	75
10/	Interrupted Plans	93
11/	Rungs on the Ladder	104
12/	Doing the Impossible	119

INTRODUCTION

Question: What is success? How do you define it?

In each area of life or work there are different symbols for it. To the writer, it is a best-selling book or the Pulitzer Prize. To the architect, it may be the MAME award. To the soldier, it may be a general's stars. To the businessman, it may be a million dollars. Most Americans still hold the dream of owning their own home, maybe a vacation home, too. To them, that may be success.

There are books, cassette tapes, and videos on the market today that all purport to have the keys to success within their framework. Most of them talk about believing in yourself, working hard, being in the right place at the right time, or knowing the right people. But what value system do all of those books, tapes, and videos hold? Which "sultan of success" do you follow? Is there more to winning and being a winner than liking yourself, believing in yourself, depending upon yourself?

Unequivocally, YES!

These equations tell you the key is within yourself. But humanism is not the answer. For if you look to a fallen man, with a fallen nature, with fallen and fallacious reasoning, decision-making abilities, and corrupted dreams, the end result cannot be anything except a fallen, fallacious, corrupted conclusion.

So where do you look? Should a Christian seek to win? Does it always have to be at the world's definition and pace?

Unequivocably, NO!

There is a lasting system of values standing authoritatively over every issue of life. There *is* an absolute standard. There is a definition for success that is within the realm of the achievable for everyone.

No. It's not in someone's book on *101 Ways to Achieve Success and Influence People.* It's found in the only infallible Book in the world.

Do not let this Book of the Law depart from your mouth; meditate on it day and night, so that you may be careful to do everything written in it. Then you will be prosperous and successful.

Have I not commanded you? Be strong and courageous. Do not be terrified; do not be discouraged, for the Lord your God will be with you wherever you go.

(Joshua 1:8-9)

Let's explore real success. Discover how to be a winner—God's way.

Chapter 1/
The Winner's Edge

Loser. Winner.

Two words. Opposite ends of an emotional and psychological spectrum. Let's look at a few "accepted" notions about each.

Loser. No one likes a loser, hopeless, incompetent.

Winner. Accolades, cheering crowds, ticker-tape parades.

Loser. Skid row, welfare, food stamps, jobless.

Winner. Success, power, money, influence.

Is the world this black and white? Is there more to life than these two terms? Do the terms need to be redefined?

The desire to win and to feel good about yourself is several thousand years old. Actually, the realization of what it means to win or lose sprang into full bloom in the Garden of Eden. When Adam and Eve disobeyed the Lord God and ate of the fruit of the knowledge of good and evil, they suddenly, irrevocably knew through bitter experience what it meant to lose—and to lose big.

Ever since that grim day, man has had to seek a new standard. The constant search for "the winning edge" has haunted his every endeavor. It is something we are taught to crave almost from the cradle. We are convinced that "no one likes a loser." "Be all that you can be" rings vigorously in our ears. And when you feel like you are losing, it seems as if everyone else is winning and that the ticker-tape parades are passing you by.

Winning. It can be frustrating, exhilarating, depressing,

satisfying, godly, or ungodly. The desire to win can make or break you depending upon the system of values you allow to mold your life. God gives us the privilege of success, but it is always on His terms and in His ways. Sometimes that means a quiet, simple life filled with heartache and sacrifice. It may mean looking like a failure in the world's eyes because you reject unethical ways to "make it big." It may mean becoming the steward of millions of dollars, properties, and businesses. It may mean having an astute mind that sees quickly and incisively into matters—and using that ability to help, not hurt.

The Bible declares that, "Heaven and earth will pass away, but my words will never pass away" (Matthew 24:35). It is in meditating and studying God's Word that we avoid the pitfalls of the world's definition of success and walk safely through the quicksand heralded by the siren song of "win at any cost."

But we need to take heart in our journey to success. Before Joshua could lead a ragtag troop of untrained, desert weary Hebrews into a luscious valley of milk and honey, he, too, had to learn and live God's definition of success. Joshua knew that winning came only from being everything *God* wanted him to be and doing only what *He* wanted him to do. It's the same for us.

There *is* much more to life than the descriptions above.

We can be successful in a career, and totally fail in our personal lives. We can make $75,000 a year, but be so far from God that life is empty and meaningless.

Put the scalpel of honest introspection to your life. Without the use of emotional anesthesia, answer these questions honestly from your heart.

1. Is Jesus Christ truly first in my life?

2. Do my personal life, relationships, job, thoughts, home, and actions reflect that commitment?
3. In what ways can I say "yes"? In what areas do I have to say "no"?
4. Is God pleased with my life?

If you need an extra pair of hands to stop the bleeding, the Great Physician is on call twenty-four hours a day with His very special balm of healing. He even has a prescription for the pain. It's in His Word. And God does make house calls.

Chapter 2/ Positive Perspectives

It's early in the morning and you find yourself once again slipping into conscious reality. It's the most wonderful time of the day for there are no sounds...except the belligerent ticking of the clock.

Then it happens! The alarm blares, splitting the still silence into a thousand pieces. Switching the alarm clock off with semi-firmness of mind and body, you ease out of bed. The world hears from your own lips the kind of person you are. Is it: "It's morning again!" or, "Is it morning...again?"

Our speech reveals our motivations. There are many people who look at half a glass of water and see it as half empty. Others view it as half full. That personal perspective reveals a lot about us. Throughout the Scriptures, we find that a personal, positive perspective is of critical importance. Look at Joshua 1:6-9 again.

Be strong and courageous, because you will lead these people to inherit the land I swore to their forefathers to give them. Be strong and very courageous. Be careful to obey all the law my servant Moses gave you; do not turn from it to the right or to the left, that you may be successful wherever you go. . . .Have not I commanded you? Be strong and courageous.

Before God sent Joshua to accomplish great things for the soon-to-be kingdom of Israel, He repeated a certain phrase to him three different times:

"Be strong and very courageous."

Anytime God repeats Himself, especially within a few verses, listen intently!

Joshua needed to hear those words. He had seen God do miracles in Moses' life and in the general assembly of Israel. But apart from the gift of life itself, the miracles of God were virtually absent in his life. Though acquainted with a winner and playing on a winning team, he was not one himself. . .yet! At least not visibly.

But make no mistake about it. God expected Joshua to do his very best. It was no half-hearted effort God was asking of Joshua. And God knew that what He was expecting of Joshua would be hard. Hard enough for Joshua to need to hear those words several times.

"Be strong and very courageous."

We don't need a lot of strength or courage for the easy tasks. God was saying, "Joshua, believe in yourself just like I believe in you. And believe in Me."

All winners have a strong, positive perspective of life that flows from the Holy Spirit within, driving them to godly success. Only after believing in ourselves, in who we are in Christ, do we have the courage to reach for that illusive brass ring on the merry-go-round of life. That perspective is a pulse beat, an electrical surge of power supercharged from the King of Kings and Lord of Lords. Get in a crowd of people like that, and you'll find yourself caught up with the excitement of expectation. But associate with people who insist life is rotten and unfair, and you'll soon find yourself expecting to lose. Anytime we blame anything or anyone else for what's happening or not happening in our lives, we've accepted the world's excuses and limited the working of God in our lives.

What about the individual with a negative outlook whose cup is always half empty? Drink from their supply long enough and you'll experience emotional indigestion with nothing to "spell relief." Positive affirmation always reproduces itself in others. Spend time with someone who believes in himself and enjoys each breath of life. His attitude is infectious. You'll soon laugh like he does and maybe even find yourself using his same upbeat vocabulary. People with positive attitudes are a joy to be around because they see the positive even in negative situations. Emotional cloning can work because most often positive people see God's hand in life whether the clouds are dark and heavy or light and breezy.

The story is told of a very successful man who was asked to what he credited his success. "Good judgment," was the reply. "To what do you attribute your good judgment?" was the next question. He answered, "Experience." "Then to what do you attribute your experience?" With a chuckle, he said, "Poor judgment!"

We can learn from negative situations. Christ spoke most eloquently to Simon Peter in his failures. It was only then that He had Peter's full attention.

By rejecting the natural tendency to slip into negativism, we catapult ourselves into the same mindset that the Lord sought to instill in Moses, Joshua, David, Peter, Paul, and Barnabas. God is not a god of the negative. He is positive and powerful. Remember II Timothy 1:7?

For God did not give us a spirit of timidity, but a spirit of power, of love and of self-discipline.

When you became a child of God, you became a winner. You had all the ingredients of success poured into you. You gained the winning edge the moment you became a Christian. But the painful part is learning to redefine success. The negative seedbed of discouragement must be attacked with the powerful antidote of God's Word, especially when you're up against unbeatable odds and uncrossable rivers. Remember Elizabeth, the cousin of Mary? When the angel told her she would have a baby in her old age, the accompanying word was, "For nothing is impossible with God" (Luke 1:37). Luke 18:27 reminds us, "What is impossible with men is possible with God."

During the Civil War, after a day of tremendous losses for the Union, General Grant was approached by his Chief of Staff, McPherson. "General, we have lost half of our artillery and a third of our men. Our lines are broken, and we are pushed back to the river! What shall we do?" "Do?" inquired the General. "Reform the lines and attack at daybreak! Won't they be surprised!" And surprised they were.

God wants to teach us to take negative situations in hand and screen them through a personal, positive, godly perspective, creating the foundation of success. Every negative thing that happens in your life is one of God's building blocks. It might be part of your character God needs to do some work on. It can be a springboard to a greater opportunity, not a diving board into despair. But it is up to us to see every incident as a gateway opened by the hand of God, our loving heavenly Father. Unless we develop a positive mentality in life and begin to move forward, we will stay where we are and emotionally stagnate. Disaster and fear are the rancid fruit of the man who dies within, refusing to believe in himself or in the God who indwells him. When we accept a negative attitude, we are really denying the power and sovereignty of God in our lives. We are saying that God is not able. And that is always the first step on the ladder downward—to the accompaniment of satanic glee. It is Satan, our arch-enemy and the arch-enemy of God, who engineers those feelings of despair.

Many people have been afflicted with LSE: Low (or

Lost) Self-Esteem. What it really is is a misplaced sense of who they are in Christ and the Christ who lives in them. Many grow up with the "loser's" mentality in their lives. Over and over again they repeat to themselves words that destroy, not build up. They refuse to grow up in Christ and subsequently fall victim to a remorseless world system ruled by their worst enemy: Satan.

I'll never forget an elderly man in the first church I served as pastor. Though a faithful deacon, he refused to sing any hymn or chorus. Not once did I ever see him even try to make a "joyful noise." In fact, there was never any noise from his lips at all. Burdened by his lack of praise in the musical part of our worship services, I asked him one day why he didn't sing. I was astounded by the answer.

"Pastor," he said, "when I was young, I loved to sing. We had a piano at the house, and every evening we children would gather around and sing as Mom played. My three sisters were great vocalists. One night, as we sang, my mother stopped playing and said, 'You can't sing, son, so just listen to your sisters.' Pastor, I have never sung a note since."

Whether the lad could sing or not, I don't know. But I do know that his mother instilled in her eight-year-old son the conviction that he couldn't sing, and he never sang again. A year after our conversation, he passed away. I have no doubt he's in heaven with Jesus finding out that he *can* sing with new words of praise at every note.

Admittedly, there may be an occasional person motivated to success by negative words.

Gregor Piatigorsky, the famous cellist, was practicing during the last few minutes before a concert with Toscanini. While in the practice room, as Piatigorsky prepared, Toscanini began to pace back and forth, saying over and over again, "You are no good. I am no good." Finally, the frustrated Piatigorsky said, "Please, Maestro, you are making me a nervous wreck." Turning to the cellist, Toscanini responded, "We are no good, but the others are worse. Let's go."

You do not have to put yourself, or others, down in order to achieve greatness. The Bible teaches us that we are so important that God sent His only Son, Jesus Christ, to die for our sins (John 3:16). That makes you important. That makes me important. Since God believes in us, doesn't it make sense to follow His example?

Remember:
All winners have a personal, positive perspective of themselves as a child of God.

The Apostle Paul had the greatest built-in success image our world has ever known. If Paul had been in the insurance business, he would have been in the "Million Dollar Club" within six months. More prolific in his writing than any other apostle, the inspired sage penned several incomparable passages:

I can do everything through him who gives me strength. (Philippians 4:13).

What, then, shall we say in response to this? If God is for us, who can be against us? (Romans 8:31)

Remember God's words to Joshua?
Be strong and courageous, because you will lead these people to inherit the land I swore to their forefathers to give them. Be strong and very courageous. Be careful to obey all the law my servant Moses gave you;...Have not I

commanded you? Be strong and courageous.
(Joshua 1:6-9)

Combining the Old Testament with the New, we see another principle:

All winners have a positive perspective of their ability in Christ.

"Have not I commanded you?" Can you believe it? God was actually commanding Joshua to be prosperous and successful. But this isn't the American definition of prosperity and success. Remember, winning is both BEING and DOING all that *God* desires of you.

God promised Joshua that he could be a successful servant and know a prosperous spiritual life. Then he could be sure that what he did was God's will—and the results would be according to God's plan, honoring to God. Joshua didn't rush off on his own, with his own ideas of prosperity and success. You'll notice that there is no guarantee of health, wealth, or a trouble free life.

This was especially true of the Apostle Paul's life. Paul was convinced, as we must be, that there was nothing, literally nothing, that he could not do through the indwelling power of the Holy Spirit. Remember Philippians 4:13? Paul didn't say, "I can do all things through the Sanhedrin," or, "I can do all things through Paul of Tarsus." No. Instead, he was willing to accept the events of his life as God's will, molding him into conformity with the image of Christ. For him, that meant giving up power, prestige, even his health as he entreated the Lord to remove the thorn in his flesh (II Corinthians 12:7-9). It is also likely that he suffered from poor eyesight (Galatians 6:11). It is certain that he experienced scourgings, shipwreck, and intense discomfort (Galatians 6:17). But it was because of these "credentials" that he was among the most honored of the early Christians.

We, like Paul, are simply the channel, the conduit through which the Word flows. Christ is the One who does the winning, all the while sharing the victory with us, His children. The real winner is the one who spiritually and intellectually acknowledges that Jesus is The Power Source, his Energizer.

There are a lot of people today trying to do their best, but failing in the Christian life. "God is my helper," and "God is my co-pilot" mentalities are deeply embedded throughout Christendom. But God isn't just a "helper" or a "co-pilot." He is *the* Pilot. Why? Because it is *totally* impossible to live the Christian life apart from Christ's life in us. That's why it is called the CHRISTian life. God never planned for it to be lived in our own power.

The Christian life is a life of dependence upon Christ. Then, as we allow Him to live His life through us, we can say with the Apostle Paul, "I can do all things through Christ who strengthens me."

There is nothing that Jesus Christ can't do through me.

If you automatically say, "I can't do this," or "my church can't do that," to each new endeavor or idea, a limitation is put on Christ and His power. We never dare to go beyond where *we* can see. God's Word teaches that what is impossible with men *is* possible with God. We need to allow God to do what He does the best. . .the impossible!

Are you thinking, "Me, a success in every area of my life? That's impossible." If you are, go back and re-read this chapter. God desires to do the impossible through you just as He did through Joshua and Paul. The key? It is the personal, positive perspective that says, "I believe God can do anything through me!"

Then, when success comes, who gets the glory? God.

If you find it easy to believe in God's ability, but hard to believe in yours, listen to Paul's wise counsel:

Brothers, I do not consider myself yet to have taken hold of it. But one thing I do: Forgetting what is behind and straining toward what is ahead, I press on toward the goal to win the prize for which God has called me heavenward in Christ Jesus. (Philippians 3:13-14)

Transparent Paul. He says it again! Just what we need to hear. Too many never seek to be winners because of past battles with heavy losses. But it's a fact. You can't move forward with your eyes fixed on where you've been, especially if your past is a field of emotional land mines.

The progression of life must always be forward. We can neither live in the victories of yesterday, nor grow by brooding over yesterday's failures. Don't dwell on what you didn't accomplish. . .just press on—to win!

CHAPTER 3/
PERPLEXING SITUATIONS

We can't always solve our problems by changing circumstances. A crisis with an employer arises; what do you do? Find another job? A problem with a spouse; what do you do? Get a divorce? Sadly for some, the old adage of "jumping out of the frying pan into the fire" still prevails.

And we know that in all things God works for the good of those who love him, who have been called according to his purpose. For those God foreknew he also predestined to be conformed to the likeness of his Son, that he might be the firstborn among many brothers.
(Romans 8:28-29)

Romans 8 teaches that God uses circumstances to reshape the edges in our lives that don't look like Jesus. Tough situations only remove non-conforming features from the rough marble of our lives. When the Christian winner understands that, he can say, "*all* things work together for good."

A modern phenomena has arisen with many well-meaning Christians praising God *for* everything. But Scripture commands us to "thank God *in* all circumstances" (I Thessalonians 5:18). My parents were divorced when I was ten years old. Should I praise or thank the Lord for divorce? No, but I can praise the Lord that *through* that situation, He taught me that I could depend upon Him for all things...even a father.

It doesn't rock heaven or crack those golden streets in

glory when something difficult happens in our lives. Regardless of what caused it, our Father knew it would happen. He has allowed it, but what you do with that "situation" determines the outcome of your life's story. The Father wants us to trust Him, to lean on Him, to let Him guide us through the valleys. It's when we ignore His outstretched hand that we stumble.

Think about it. Where is the battleground in the war of mind *versus* situation? Between the ears! Our thoughts have a direct relationship to our physical campaigns in life. *If you lose in the head, you lose in life.*

We might as well acknowledge it now: *LIFE IS NOT ALWAYS FAIR!* Jesus said it this way: "In this world you will have trouble" (John 16:33b). He also said, "But take heart! I have overcome the world." In Matthew 5:44-45 He said, "But I tell you, Love your enemies and pray for those who persecute you, that you may be sons of your Father in heaven. He causes his sun to rise on the evil and the good, and sends rain on the righteous and the unrighteous."

From a prison cell, the Apostle Paul wrote:

"Yes, and I will continue to rejoice, for I know that through your prayers and help given by the Spirit of Jesus Christ, what has happened to me will turn out for my deliverance." (Philippians 1:18b-19)

Paul left that jail cell to go to his execution. But in spite of that overwhelming possibility, his life evidenced a constant, godly perspective of the situation. He knew to whom he had committed his life and that trust was unwavering. It affected and guided his entire perspective of life and his circumstances.

Perplexing situations, like the days of our lives, come and go. Some days we're on top; some days we're not! In fact, our situation may change for bad as fast as it did for good—or vice versa. A godly outlook must be guarded at all times and consciously nurtured. But how do you do that? Write it! Sing it! Say it! Read it in Paul's personal history: "I have learned the secret of being content in any and every situation, whether well-fed or hungry, whether living in plenty or in want" (Philippians 4:12).

So you find yourself with no food? Dream diet! The contemporary proverb says, "When life hands you a lemon, make lemonade!" That positive attitude in all situations will define you as a winner, or, if absent, declare you a loser.

I love the story of two shoe salesmen who were transferred to Africa. The first, after getting off the plane, sent a cable back to the home office requesting a transfer immediately. The reason? "No one wears shoes in Africa!" However, the other bounded off the airplane and sent a cable home just as fast. It read: "Send everything in stock! No one wears shoes!"

What was the difference? A positive perspective of the situation. You may not have control over the circumstances, but you can control your attitude.

"My life has been filled with terrible things—most of which never happened," was the perspective of a wise philosopher. It's often prevalent in the lives of those we know—or in our own. Have you ever noticed the great number of people who are so down on life that they can't see the blue sky and hear the birds sing? They are blind, insensitive to the sights and sounds of the world God gave them to enjoy (I Timothy 6:17). Focusing on what they see as disaster or difficulties, they are blind to God's hand and His working in their lives.

Some years ago, a young woman was found crying bitterly. "What's wrong?" asked her friend. "You're so brokenhearted. What on earth happened to you?" Pointing to the well in the middle of the field in which they were standing, she said, "I was just sitting here thinking that one day I might get asked out for a date. Then I might accept. I might eventually fall in love with the fellow and become engaged. After that, we might get married and have a few children. They might even play out here in this field. One day, one of them might come out here to this well, lean over, and fall in...oh, boo hoo, boo hoo!"

Imaginary problems, bridges crossed before the journey's begun, and mental "mights" handicap would-be winners by robbing us of the freedom to truly enjoy our God-given right to *His* positive perspective of our lives.

Remember Paul. A dungeon living room decorated with muted light and a catering service committed to "weight loss" were his physical surroundings. The neighbors in his part of Rome were less than socially acceptable. If anybody had a right to be angry or depressed at life—or God—it was Paul. But did he complain? Read for yourself as his poignant pen with Holy Spirit empowered ink lifted others in Philippi and us today.

Convinced of this, I know that I will remain, and I will continue with all of you for your progress and joy in the faith, so that through my being with you again your joy in Christ Jesus will overflow on account of me!

(Philippians 1:25-26)

Can you believe it? This is the portrait of a man in a terrible situation. What do you notice in the picture, though? Joy!

The word "joy" is used over twenty-five times by Paul in his epistle to the Philippians. What motivates a man in a situation as desperate as Paul's to be filled with joy? Did he do the mental push-ups that the superstar salesmen's rallies conjure up? I can see it now...Paul walking around the dirt and straw floor in the prison cell calling forth positive emotion by repeating, "I feel great! I feel great! I'm going to win! I feel great!"

I don't think so.

So why was he filled with joy? His relationship to Jesus Christ was the key to his perspective. It didn't depend upon emotions, feelings, or circumstances. The believer's enthusiasm which attracts the world does not have to be artificially induced; it comes from the Lord.

"Enthusiasm." Break the word down. "En" and "theos" are Greek words forming the concept "in God." And the exciting joy of enthusiasm comes from union with God through salvation in Jesus Christ.

I have found that people are not drawn to the church because of the buildings; the world has even more majestic and beautiful buildings. It is also true that the world will never be drawn to the church only because of music because the world has many different kinds of beautiful music. Personalities and programs will not do it either for the world has those, also. However, if the church recaptures the joy described in Acts 1 at Pentecost, the world will be captivated.

The joy of Pentecost was not in the wind or in the tongues of fire. It was not even in the hundreds who heard the message. Where was it? It was God in man for the very first time, the Holy Spirit living in yielded believers. That experience of God indwelling man produced boldness to proclaim, create, touch, reach, and to succeed. The church was born and winning values were created in those who followed Christ.

Imagine the thousands of believers, eyes popping open that morning following Pentecost as they jumped out of bed, ready to take the world by storm. Instead of fear, anxiety, depression, or even apathy, they were filled with a positive, personal faith and attitude toward life, any situation, and their ability in Christ for they were born-again to be winners—on Christ's terms. The first words that came from their lips? "Good morning, Lord!" Convinced that they were winners, they dared to risk everything the world held dear—even their lives. They knew that in Christ they couldn't lose anything that really mattered.

CHAPTER 4/
PERSISTENT PRIORITIES

> But Moses said, "Why are you disobeying the Lord's command? This will not succeed! Do not go up, because the Lord is not with you. You will be defeated by your enemies, for the Amalekites and Canaanites will face you there. Because you have turned away from the Lord, he will not be with you and you will fall by the sword." Nevertheless, in their presumption, they went up toward the high hill country, though neither Moses or the Ark of the Lord's covenant moved from the camp. Then the Amalekites and Canaanites who lived in that hill country came down and attacked them and beat them down all the way to Hormah.
>
> (Numbers 14:41-45)

The Israelites were on a winning streak. Leaving Egypt in a huge parade, carrying the spoils of Pharaoh's coffers with them, they experienced no opposition until the Egyptian potentate realized what he had done. Millions of his slaves were headed north on the Egyptian turnpike straight for the State line. He and his army mounted and went after them. But the Israelites could not be stopped.

Splitting the Red Sea, God provided deliverance and destroyed Pharaoh's army with a simple command and the obedience of Moses. In the midst of their wilderness travel, God took care of them physically. Appetizers of manna followed by quail over wild rice were served daily.

Comfortable accommodations with a heavenly lighting system were given to them. A pillar of fire supplied central heating at night and a cloud led them confidently during the day.

They couldn't lose. . .or could they?

The Hebrew Winner's Rally was stopped dead in its tracks by a small group of "ites." Even though they were God's chosen people, the Hebrews encountered failure. They learned that yesterday's conquests do not guarantee today's success or tomorrow's victory.

What, then, makes a winner? What separates the victors from the vanquished? Scripture reveals certain characteristics evident in the lives of true winners.

In the previous chapter, we saw that winners need a positive, godly perspective. Although the Israelites knew they would ultimately defeat their enemies, experience taught them a valuable lesson. Confidence was not enough to claim victory. Why? Because they had failed at another critical characteristic of winning: *All winners have certain persistent priorities.*

Just because you are a child of God does not mean that you will succeed every time, at everything you attempt. If you follow the history of the Israelites through the Old Testament, you will find these same chosen people wandering aimlessly in the wilderness for over forty years, experiencing more failure than success. Observation points out the lack of certain enduring priorities in the Hebrews.

Defeat and despair were not to last long in Israel's history, though. Four kings of Israel—godly men embodying certain godly characteristics—stepped onto the stage. Five "one-liners" from the lives of Israel's heroes describe the persistent priorities each winner must possess.

Play these kings' roles in the drama of your life. Step onto center stage as you practice and perform the first of these five key traits. Say it out loud:

"I WILL SEEK THE LORD."

Enter King Uzziah. Beginning his reign at the age of sixteen, Jerusalem experienced fifty-two years of his wonderful rule. The biblical writer reveals Uzziah's secret of successful kingship.

He sought God during the days of Zechariah, who instructed him in the fear of God. As long as he sought the Lord, God gave him success. (II Chronicles 26:5)

Enter King Hezekiah. He had the same priority.

This is what Hezekiah did throughout Judah, doing what was good and right and faithful before the Lord his God. In everything that he undertook in the service of God's temple and in obedience to the law and the commands, he sought his God and worked wholeheartedly. And so he prospered. (II Chronicles 31:20-21)

Next we see King Jehoshaphat seeking the Lord.

The Lord was with Jehoshaphat because in his early years he walked in the ways his father David had followed. He did not consult the Baals but sought the God of his father and followed his commands rather than the practices of Israel. (II Chronicles 17:3-4)

Then we see the spotlight of Scripture highlight King Asa.

Asa did what was good and right in the eyes of the Lord his God. He removed the foreign altars and the high places, smashed the sacred stones and cut down the Asherah poles. He commanded Judah to seek the Lord,

> *the God of their fathers, and to obey his laws and commands. He removed the high places and incense altars in every town in Judah, and the kingdom was at peace under him. He built up the fortified cities of Judah, since the land was at peace. No one was at war with him during those years, for the Lord gave him rest.*
>
> *"Let us build up these towns," he said to Judah, "and put walls around them, with towers, gates and bars. The land is still ours, because we have sought the Lord our God; ... and he has given us rest on every side." So they built and prospered.* (II Chronicles 14:2-7)

Just like these kings, to become a winner, we must remove any foreign altars in our lives and consistently seek the Lord. When we rely on an organization, we get only what an organization can do—even if that organization is the church. If we rest on education, we receive only what education can do—head knowledge without heart knowledge. Lean on personality, and we get only what personality can do.

But when we pray, seeking the Lord, we experience what only God can do. Winners are those who, when finding themselves surrounded by impossible situations, turn *to* God in prayer, not away from Him.

Prayer is the first step in seeking God. And God answers prayer in several ways. Sometimes He says, in contemporary terms, "Go for it!" or "No way!" Often He says, "Slow down."

Other times He just changes our minds. The old story is told of a little boy who lost a marble. Disturbed by the loss, his mother noticed that he could not focus his mind on his work. Suddenly, he asked, "Mom, can I ask God to help me find my marble?" Giving her consent, she allowed the little boy to kneel by his chair, watching him as his eyes closed in silent prayer. He then arose and went on contentedly with his lessons. The next day, with a hint of hesitancy, she inquired, "Well, son, have you found your marble yet?"

"No," came the reply, "but God has made me not want to anymore."

As we seek the Lord, we can be sure that we can trust Him. When we can commit our desires to the Lord with that same kind of faith, our success becomes His success—and His success ours.

Now we're ready for the second priority—this time from a Hebrew hero, Joshua.

"I WILL LISTEN TO THE LORD."

The Lord told Joshua—and through him us—to pay close attention to His Word.

Be strong and courageous, because you will lead these people to inherit the land I swore to their forefathers to give them. Be strong and very courageous. Be careful to obey all the law my servant Moses gave you; do not turn from it to the right or to the left, that you may be successful wherever you go. Do not let this Book of the law depart from your mouth; meditate on it day and night, so that you may be careful to do everything written in it. Then you will be prosperous and successful. (Joshua 1:7-8)

Who do you go to when you are perplexed by life? How do you know what God wants for your life? How do you know what step to take next? How do you determine which desire in your life is trustworthy? The Bible is not just a book about heaven, nor does it record only sobering words concerning the reality of hell.

It is *the Book*, guiding believers to victory in every area of life. It is through reading, meditating, and memorizing the Word of God that a Christian can know the right direction for his life and see his goals attained. It is when our goals and the means of accomplishing them are fine-tuned to the Bible's standards that we find godly prosperity and success.

For instance? Contemplating marriage? God says, "Do not be yoked together with unbelievers." Tempted to "fudge" a little on the income tax returns? "Submit yourselves for the Lord's sake to every authority instituted among men.... For it is God's will that by doing good you should silence the ignorant talk of foolish men" (I Peter 2:13,15). Angry at someone who has hurt you? "Do not repay anyone evil for evil....Do not take revenge, my friends.... Overcome evil with good" (Romans 12:17-21). When we live according to the standards, principles, and commands of God's Word, then we become successful in a way the world cannot even comprehend.

Dr. Charles Elliott was a lifelong Bible student. Just a month before his death at age 77, he read the Old Testament through in only three weeks. One day as he read, his daughter asked him what he was reading. "News," he replied, "news."

Don't read the Bible as a history book, or just for devotional material. It is both, but it is also much more. The psalmist stated it this way: "Your word is a lamp to my feet and a light for my path" (Psalm 119:105). The Bible is a guidebook, revealing our exact position and, at the same time, charting our course with heavenly accuracy, compassion, wisdom, and love.

Have you found yourself off course on your way to success? Reach for the Bible, God's compass for His people.

Did you know that it only takes an average of seventy hours and forty minutes to read the Bible? Of that, it takes fifty-two hours and twenty minutes to read the Old Testament and eighteen hours, twenty minutes to read the New Testament. In the Old Testament, the Psalms take the longest to read: four hours and twenty-eight minutes. In the New Testament, the Gospel of Luke takes two hours and forty-three minutes to read. In comparison to the amount of time we spend watching television or in recreational activities, giving an equal amount of time to reading the Bible should be no problem at all. It's just a matter of priorities.

Perhaps the greatest priority that we can have on this side of eternity is *to listen to the Lord.* All winners make listening to the Lord a persistent priority. Then, God's will is always accomplished.

"...So is my word that goes out from my mouth: it will not return to me empty, but will accomplish what I desire and achieve the purpose for which I sent it."

(Isaiah 55:11)

You probably have a radio or television in your home. Even with the switch in the "off" position, there are songs being played, words spoken, and pictures projected. Why can't you hear them? Why can't you see them? The answer is simple: You have not utilized the power source. You are not tuned to the right station. The same is true with God. If we are not connected to Him as our power source, then we'll never hear God's message. Sometimes the only way He can get our attention is to broadcast on our emergency broadcasting system! Stay tuned to God's channel, the Bible. The emergencies won't surprise or hurt you as much.

Joshua has another priority to be memorized by the true winner.

"I WILL OBEY THE LORD."

When it comes to winning, obedience always follows listening. Had the Israelites heeded Moses' word about faithful worship (Exodus 24:1-8), they would have saved their lives as well as their reputations. It is not enough to seek and to listen to God. We must *do* what He says. Obedience is everything!

When General Montgomery directed the Allied Forces in North Africa during World War II, he inherited a losing situation. A practice had developed under other leadership that once a command was given, the subordinates questioned it all the way down the line. After taking countless losses, investigation revealed the practice to be the key to their defeats. General Montgomery issued the ultimatum: "From now on, all orders are to be followed without question—immediately!"

The same is true for Christians. We cannot afford the luxury of heavenly negotiation and expect to win. Remember, if you're too far away from God to hear His voice, there is no way to obey His orders.

The children of Israel were defeated, not because they were militarily unable, but because they disobeyed God. They had seen God work miracles. They often sought His words and listened to His prophet's instructions. But one thing was missing: obedience. Real winners obey the Lord. "Does the Lord delight in burnt offerings and sacrifices as much as in obeying the voice of the Lord? To obey is better than sacrifice, and to heed is better than the fat of rams" (I Samuel 15:22).

King Hezekiah, not to be outdone by the general who conquered Jericho, captures the essence of a winner with yet another priority:

"I AM HOLDING FAST TO THE LORD."

Hezekiah trusted in the Lord, the God of Israel. There was no one like him among all the kings of Judah, either before him or after him. He held fast to the Lord and did not cease to follow Him; he kept the commands the Lord had given Moses. And the Lord was with him; he was successful in whatever he undertook. (II Kings 18:5-7)

Think about it! Wouldn't you like to be successful in everything you attempted? It is possible. The secret to that kind of success is located in the heart of this passage.

". . .He held fast to the Lord and did not cease to follow Him." It is this persistent priority that carries the believer to the threshold of victory. If you desire to be a real winner, hold fast to the Lord.

How do you do that? The answer is found in the Old Testament as well as the New. "Delight yourself *in the Lord* (emphasis mine) and He will give you the desires of your heart" (Psalm 37:4). Many try to make that a *carte blanche* from the Lord. But it isn't. What does that verse mean? Simply, make Him the center of your life, allowing Him to become your life. Can you imagine the Lord craving that imported luxury car or that big, new house? With Job, learn to say instead, "Though He slay me, I will trust Him" (Job 13:15). Regardless of the circumstances or what happens in your life, hold on to the Father. As a vine wraps itself around a tree, wrap yourself around the Lord. Say with the Apostle Paul, "I have learned to be content whatever the circumstances" (Philippians 4:11).

Walk with God daily, moment-by-moment. Keep Him in the center of your mental eyesight. Fill you heart and thoughts with rejoicing and thankfulness. Don't let your thoughts focus on the negatives. Rather, concentrate on all the good in your life—even if the only item you can think of at the moment is the fact that you are a child of the King and loved by the Creator of the universe. After all, that's pretty terrific!

It shouldn't surprise us that God holds fast to us, too. The moment we invite Jesus to be our Savior, He comes to live inside of us, desiring us to hold fast to Him as He holds us in the palm of His hand (John 10:29).

Now we're ready for that last essential priority. Remember each one who entered the stage of life to declare various priorities? Now the entire cast is center stage in front of the stage lights. Together they declare:

"I AM TRUSTING THE LORD."

Regardless of how impossible, ridiculous, dangerous, or unlikely the request or direction God gave His men, those who were to be real winners always stepped out on faith, completely trusting God as evidenced by their obedience. Abram, Joshua, Hezekiah, Asa, Jehoshaphat, Uzziah, and even the New Testament apostle, Paul, experienced incredible success as they trusted God. And God recorded their faithfulness and obedience for us—as examples and encouragement.

I'm still amazed at how God orchestrated the defeat of Jericho under the leadership of Joshua. It took a real man of God, a real winner, to risk ridicule by leading the people in a parade around the city for seven days, and, on the seventh day, to parade around seven times. Then, as the band began to play, everybody shouted and the walls came tumbling down. Not a weapon was raised. Not a Hebrew man lost his life. Strange war plans, but Joshua was God's general, and he trusted the Lord with his life and the lives of his countrymen. Acting on those puzzling strategy plans proved that Joshua trusted God.

God wants us to take similar steps of faith as we allow Him to direct our lives—our "battle plans" for Monday morning, for next week, for our relationships, for our lives. It means knowing God's plans through studying

Redefining Success

His "strategy manual," the Bible, and letting go of our own plans and abilities, confident that the Father's are much better.

In the early fifties, a radio announcer asked Leo Durocher, manager of the New York Giants, "Barring the unforeseen, Leo, will your club win the pennant?" Durocher's reply came quickly. "There ain't gonna be no unforeseen."

When we trust the God of all creation, there won't be anything unforeseen—to Him. As potential winners, we have one of two choices: to trust ourselves and have incomplete enjoyment and some worldly fulfillment in life, or, to take a giant step of faith and become a full-fledged winner by trusting in the Lord. As believers, we're on a pilgrimage where the road is sometimes frightful, often alarming, sometimes unseen, but always exciting. Get a glimpse of the sheer, vibrant adventure that following the Lord ensures.

One dark and stormy night, (all great stories begin like that!) the passengers on a speeding train were uneasy as they raced along the tracks. The lightning was flashing and thunder shook the cars. Fear and mounting tension swept through the passenger compartments. One of the frightened travelers noticed a little boy sitting alone, apparently utterly unaware of the storm or even the speed of the train. He was calmly amusing himself with his little toys. The concerned observer, in a fright-filled voice, said, "Sonny, aren't you afraid to travel alone on such a treacherous, fearful night?" The little boy just looked up at him with a smile and answered, "No, sir, I'm not afraid. My daddy is the engineer."

Who's running your life? Take a moment to reflect on the last week. Is Jesus Christ the engineer sitting at the controls, handling the crisis? Is He the executive producer

and director of every scene in your life?
Are these the persistent priorities in your life?
- I will seek the Lord.
- I will listen to the Lord.
- I will obey the Lord.
- I am holding fast to the Lord.
- I am trusting the Lord.

CHAPTER 5/ PERSONAL PURITY

> Surely the arm of the Lord is not too short to save, nor his ear too dull to hear. But your iniquities have separated you from your God; your sins have hidden his face from you, so that he will not hear.
> (Isaiah 59:1-2)

Stranded! Mike Turner and I were stranded on foot on a sandbar in the back bay of Cedar Cut, off the Texas coast. It was 2 a.m. and our lanterns would soon lose their light because our fuel was slowly, relentlessly dwindling. Seeking flatfish, commonly known as flounder, we found ourselves hopelessly trapped as the tide began to roll in from the rising sea. Endless searching for the path to the other side of the bay produced nothing, except to add more panic to our already huge supply. I was scared! I didn't mind admitting it.

We had traveled hours just to use the darkness of night as a cover to gig flounder for a fish-fry. Soon the light of morning would arrive, and we would meet it drowned, "skunked," or both. Thousands of tons of water prevented us from doing what we had planned to do for six months: gig flounder. It looked like our planned trip would turn out a disaster, rather than a success.

I said, "Mike, follow me. I'll get us off this sandbar!" So, like a good friend, he followed until frustration caused him to say, "Curt, follow me. You don't know where you're going." He was right. I didn't. But, neither did he!

We spent an hour following each other's ignorant intentions. It was the blind leading the blind. We looked at each other and finally admitted, "We're in trouble!" The water kept rising, but not as high as our anxiety.

Finally, we saw another lantern light on the other side of the sandbar. It was Doug Cochran, a member of our party who knew the area like it was his back yard. We calmly yelled, "Get us off this sandbar!" He laughed and then came for us, knowing how to cross the channel. Were we glad to see him! Following Doug proved to be the key to success for he, alone, knew the way off the sandbar. Soon, it was light and our fishing expedition was over. We had nothing to show for it except eight small fish and a restored sense of peace and safety.

Stranded...I'll never forget that feeling! Added to it, I was prevented from accomplishing my goal. What a frustrating night!

Much like a rising tide flowing through a deep, saltwater channel, sin separates us from success in our Christian lives.

Biblical history reveals that when the channel of sin was crossed and personal purity and commitment established, success was inevitable. In God's Word, all winners were only truly successful when they were right before God and in constant communication with Him (Romans 12:1-2; I Thessalonians 5:17). The Bible teaches that unconfessed sin flows into the back bays of our lives, separating us from God.

How do you know if you're spiritually stranded? Answer these questions and find out.

How's your prayer life?

Is your hotline to heaven a direct line, or do you have to go through directory assistance to find the number for the throne?

Have you ever felt like your prayers didn't get above the ceiling? Maybe your feelings were right because there was unconfessed sin in your life, blocking your fellowship (Psalm 66:18; John 9:31, 15:7; James 4:2-3,8).

During my seminary days, Bertha Smith, a retired missionary from China, spoke to my Missionary Preparation class. Pointing her finger at the young seminarians with words that cut through my heart like the blade of a knife, she asked: "Boys, are your sins confessed up-to-date?" That question has never left my mind. It is only when our "sins are confessed up-to-date" that pure living and a direct line of communication between *us* and *God* occurs.

That line of communication flows the other way as well. Living a pure life opens the line of communication between *God* and *us*. In communication, there are two basic things that must be remembered. There is "what is being said" and "what is being perceived." It is in that area of perception that many stumble on their way to success. Either there is a misinterpretation of God's guidance or a lack of spiritual reception on the believer's part.

Sometimes we get preoccupied, living down in the cellar of life, burdened and captivated by the bondage of sin in the devil's dungeon of despair. When God communicates with us, His voice is muffled through the sinful wax in our spiritual ears.

One of the advantages of a pure life is its provision for the maximum avenue of peace. Our world is looking for that peace, but it only occurs when personal, godly purity becomes a priority in our lives.

Throughout its pages, the Bible teaches us that personal purity is measured by God's standards. When we think about God's standards, most of us think about the Ten Commandments, those ten moral and ethical laws upon which all of civilization is based. Jesus took it a step further when He said purity is proved by the motives of your heart (I Corinthians 3:10-15, 18-23). If we hate our brother, we are guilty of murder (I John 3:15). The Bible declares if you have sinned or broken one part of the law, you have broken it all (James 2:10). The Bible says, "The whole world is a prisoner of sin" (Galatians 3:22), and we are captivated by sin as it drags us down. God's Word clearly reveals to us that we are sinners. "For all have sinned and fall short of the glory of God" (Romans 3:23). Let's admit it: our world has a sin problem. Not only is Satan the princely ruler of it (Ephesians 2:1-3), but it is filled with unregenerate human beings.

The biblical word for sin is a simple one. It means "to miss the mark." So, let's face it. Compared to God's standards of purity, we haven't even hit the target, much less the bull's-eye. And that standard has never changed!

I have found it very interesting that every time I speak to an audience about personal sin, the crowd gets quiet. It never fails. Scripture declares that God's requirements are written on our hearts and even our thoughts accuse us (Romans 2:15). Unfailingly, we recognize it when confronted.

Our personal purity is not to be measured by someone else or their failures, either. Why? There will always be another person better than you, as well as worse than you. But, that's not the real problem! The real reason is that God holds each of us personally accountable (Romans 14:9-13). What someone else has done holds no importance to God when He's evaluating our life and service.

God not only declares that we should live holy as He is holy (I Peter 1:15-16), but He provides that motivation to be holy. God the Holy Spirit, who indwells the believer, urges each of us to live a pure life from the inside out (Titus 3:5-8). Throughout His Word, He tells us how.

The moment we allow Jesus to become the Lord of our lives, He takes control, giving us new "want to's." As He reveals things in our lives that are not what He wants, He awakens us to the recognition of sin, and a desire for a personal transformation occurs. His presence in our lives motivates us to seek purity and godliness in our thoughts, words, and actions.

I've talked to hundreds of people who are convinced that they can't live a Christian life because they are unable to live up to holy standards. I must certainly agree with them and count myself among their number. We cannot live that kind of life on our own. Go ahead and admit it; say it out loud if you want. "I cannot live the Christian life." We can't; it must be an inside job. Never refuse the conviction of the Holy Spirit as He tries to change you, motivate you toward purity, and then reproduce it in your life. If we harden our hearts and refuse to change our lives to conform to the image of Christ in us, we become un-Christlike and invite God's chastisement.

Personal purity produces personal success. The lack of it, defeat. A telling example of this from Scripture is the birth and life of Samson (Judges 13). Samson was born to parents who could not have children. But the angel of the Lord appeared to her and said, "You are sterile and childless, but you are going to conceive and have a son. Now see to it that you drink no wine or other fermented drink and that you do not eat anything unclean, because you will conceive and give birth to a son. No razor may be used on his head, because the boy is to be a Nazirite, set apart to God from birth, and he will begin the deliverance of Israel from the hands of the Philistines."

Samson was to be a Nazirite. There were three things that Nazirites were prohibited from doing: First, they could neither eat nor touch any unclean thing for it caused ceremonial uncleanliness. Second, they were never to drink wine or any other fermented drink. Third, they were to let their hair grow as an outward sign of an inward spiritual vow.

In the beginning, Samson was a picture of personal purity and professional success. He was a judge of Israel and delivered the Israelites from bondage to the Philistines. The Hebrews adored Samson.

Then it happened. He began to break his Nazirite vows and tragedy soon followed. When Samson lived in purity, God gave him success. But he fell from the heights of success to the pits of failure because he rejected personal purity. Slowly, willfully, his personal life degenerated. Samson's moral failure was not a blowout, but a slow leak. Delilah was only the nail on Samson's tire that forced him out of the race.

Does that mean that just because you live a pure life that everything is going to "come up roses"? No! Daniel's life teaches us that sometimes personal purity causes problems. If you decide you are going to reject sin in your life, never willingly or knowingly giving it a resting spot in your thoughts or actions, the world is not going to love you.

Daniel was captured as a teenager, and taken to Nebuchadnezzar's Babylonian courts (Daniel 1). But even in captivity, he honored God. With three of his friends, they determined to honor the Lord God no matter what happened. God blessed their decision. They each rose to prominence within the pagan empire. Daniel eventually became chief counsel to four consecutive

Babylonian rulers even though jealous men unleashed plots to destroy him.

In one attempt, wicked men convinced King Darius that no one should pray to anybody other than to him. The penalty? Death! Daniel, because of his consistent personal purity, remained true to Yahweh. He refused to worship the king and was thrown into the lion's den (Daniel 6).

The next morning, the king rushed to the lion's den and called out to Daniel, "Daniel, servant of the living God, has your God, whom you serve continually, been able to rescue you from the lion?" And Daniel answered! "O king, live forever!" (He's still respectful.) "My God sent his angel, and he shut the mouths of the lions. They have not hurt me because I was found innocent in his sight. Nor have I ever done any wrong before you, O king" (6:20-22).

And the king was overjoyed! So overjoyed that, for breakfast, he fed his hungry lions the men who had falsely accused Daniel!

Remember Shadrach, Meshach, and Abednego? They refused to worship an image of gold, causing King Nebuchadnezzar to become furious when this slight to his pride was pointed out to him. The king had the three brought before him, questioned them, and told them their defiance meant death in a blazing furnace.

Undaunted, the three told him, "O, Nebuchadnezzar, we do not need to defend ourselves before you in this matter. If we are thrown into the blazing furnace, the God we serve is able to save us from it, and he will rescue us from your hand, O king. But *even if he does not* (emphasis mine), we want you to know, O king, that we will not serve your gods or worship the image of gold you have set up" (Daniel 3:16-18).

Now that's commitment! And in verse 28, after God did deliver them, we see a change in Nebuchadnezzar because of their unflinching commitment to God's standards. This proud king says, "Praise be to the God of Shadrach, Meshach and Abednego, who has sent his angel and rescued his servants! They trusted in him and defied the king's command and were willing to give up their lives rather than serve or worship any god except their own God." Even the king recognized the power of Daniel's God. Nebuchadnezzar's conclusion? "No other god can save in this way" (3:29).

Sometimes personal purity does produce problems, but personal purity will make sure that the lion's dens and furnaces in our lives are not of our own making. If we remain true to God, renouncing conformity to the world, we will experience His power in our lives, molding us into winners. *Never forget that*! We can resist temptation or success at the world's price if we maintain a right relationship with God.

Perhaps you are totally frustrated at this point. You didn't have to read this book to know that God measures and motivates our rejection of sinful acts and attitudes. Possibly you're even asking yourself, "Well, how in the world can it be done? How can I live a sinless life?"

One day a teacher was testing her students to find out if they knew the proverbs. She asked, "Cleanliness is next to what?" One child, without any hesitation, stood up and declared, "Impossible!" If that's what you're thinking, I've got good news for you.

When He died on Calvary's cross, Christ did two things. First, He provided the avenue through which our old sinful nature is rendered powerless. That desire to sin was nailed to the cross. And, through our acceptance of this sacrifice of His blood on the cross, we are also cleansed from sin and made clean in God's eyes (I Peter 1:18-21). Personal purity and forgiveness of sin is only possible through God's Son. Without Christ's sacrificial death on the cross, we would be forever alone, missing His presence in eternal darkness in the lake of fire (Revelation 20:15).

Feeling stranded? The rushing waters of sin do cause great fear of failure, especially when you're running low on the fuel of personal purity. Look for that lantern on the other side of the bay. The Lord Jesus Christ holds His light high to show you the only safe path from your sandbar and lead you to success.

CHAPTER 6/
INTERNAL INCENTIVES

"Not that I have already obtained all this, or have already been made perfect, but I press on to take hold of that for which Christ Jesus took hold of me. Brothers, I do not consider myself yet to have taken hold of it. But one thing I do: Forgetting what is behind and straining toward what is ahead, I press on toward the goal to win the prize for which God has called me heavenward in Christ Jesus. All of us who are mature should take such a view of things. And if on some point you think differently, that too God will make clear to you. Only let us live up to what we have already attained. Join with others in following my example, brothers, and take note of those who live according to the pattern we gave you."

(Philippians 3:12-17)

"Now, my son, the Lord be with you, and may you have success and build the house of the Lord your God, as he said you would. May the Lord give you discretion and understanding when he puts you in command over Israel, so that you may keep the law of the Lord your God. Then you will have success if you are careful to observe the decrees and laws that the Lord gave Moses for Israel. Be strong and courageous. Do not be afraid or discouraged.

(I Chronicles 22:1-13)

[King Uzziah] "sought God...who instructed him in

the fear of God. As long as he sought the Lord, God gave him success."
(II Chronicles 26:5)

"Go and inquire of the Lord for me and for the remnant in Israel and Judah about what is written in this book that has been found. Great is the Lord's anger that is poured out on us because our fathers have not kept the word of the Lord; they have not acted in accordance with all that is written in this book."
(II Chronicles 34:21)

"In everything that he [Hezekiah] undertook in the service of God's temple and in obedience to the law and the commands, he sought his God and worked wholeheartedly. And so he prospered."
(II Chronicles 31:21)

When it comes to winning and losing, there are three clearly definable groups.

First, there are individuals who CONSISTENTLY FAIL time and time again.

Their lives are filled with defeat after defeat; they never glimpse victory, only the sad news of one more failure.

Second, there are those who experience neither success nor failure, they JUST EXIST.

"Fulfillment" is not a word in their vocabulary. Of all the people upon the face of the earth, they are to be the most pitied of all. Instead of seeking to reach unbelievable heights, they risk nothing, experience little, and become even less.

Third, there are those whose lives must be labeled SUCCESSFUL—REAL WINNERS.

It seems that everything they touch turns to gold. Look up the word "excitement" in the dictionary and you'll see their picture. For most people, a dream come true in life would no doubt be to have that Winner's Touch. You and I can have that kind of success just by following the example of King Hezekiah and the Apostle Paul. Walk through their lives, practice their attributes, and become a success. They provide exciting portraits of perseverance, an essential ingredient in winning.

Anyone can work hard, but there are four mental steps that all winners take in their journey to the top. It's the war between the ears that determines how long you endure the marathon. Ninety percent of all battles for success are mental.

With the words of an athlete, Paul shows us the first step in positive, progressive perseverance:

EXAMINATION

In Philippians 3:12-13, Paul recognizes two things. First, he sees himself as he really is. He humbly acknowledged that he was not what he needed to be. But even though he knew he was not perfect, he was "pressing on" to take hold of God's best for him. Hear him say: "Brothers, I do not consider myself yet to have taken hold of it. But one thing I do: Forgetting what is behind and straining toward what is ahead, I press on. . . . All of us who are mature should take such a view of things." He was on the way to his goal by equipping himself with honest personal evaluation.

Have you done that? Open the curtains of your life and critique yourself. Observe candidly your strengths and weaknesses, failures and successes, goals and desires, the traits of your personality. Look at yourself as you really are. One who can be truly transparent with himself has nothing to fear.

Pythagoras is honored as one of the great teachers of all time. Every night he demanded that his pupils examine themselves on their progress of that particular day. They were to ask themselves four questions:

1. How did I succeed in my studies today?
2. Could I have learned more?
3. Could I have studied better?
4. Is there something I neglected?

As a result of his encouragement, his students became well-known for their learning.

It is through genuine self-examination that success can come. However, if we fail to look at ourselves as we really are, we will ultimately experience failure. In our journey to the top, one concept is critical: We cannot go to where we want to be, if we don't really know where we are. Successful forward momentum is only possible after the right direction is determined.

Where are you today? Are you where God wants you to be? Are you where you want to be? You'll never be able to answer that question until you take that first step of self-evaluation, seeing yourself as you really are. But, don't stay there—especially if it's less than encouraging!

There's a second step that you must take if you would persevere to success. Turn from introspection and examine God's best for you. See the:

GOAL

Paul penned it perfectly when he wrote, "But I press on to take hold of that for which Christ Jesus took hold of me" (Philippians 3:12). Paul saw not only himself as he really was, but also God's ultimate best for him. Paul's goal in life was the essence of winning: *Being everything God wants me to be and doing everything He wants me to do.* That ought to be the goal in each of our lives. That's what winning is.

What is God's best for you? "Now all has been heard; here is the conclusion of the matter: Fear God and keep his commandments, for this is the whole duty of man" (Ecclesiates 12:13). "Delight yourself in the Lord and he will give you the desires of your heart. Commit your way to the Lord; trust in him and he will do this: He will make your righteousness shine like the dawn, the justice of your cause like the noonday sun" (Psalm 37:4-6).

God does not create failures. They are the result of our not striving toward God's best or, conversely, of working toward man's definition of success. Everything in life reflects what we consistently perceive (Matthew 15:17-20 *cf.* Philippians 4:8). Let God brand His best on the door of your character and career.

Then, take a third step with Paul:

DETERMINATION

But one thing I do: Forgetting what is behind and

straining toward what is ahead, I press on toward the goal to win the prize for which God has called me heavenward in Christ Jesus. (Philippians 3:13-14)

Look at that first line: "But one thing I do." Determination oozes from the phrase. Paul set his mind to accomplish certain goals and achievements, all centered on God's best for his life.

However, to experience God's best, a person must be as determined as was Paul about several things.

We must be determined to forget the past. "Forgetting what is behind." Nothing will pull us down quicker than dwelling on our past. There's nothing we can do about yesterday's triumphs or mistakes. If there is a need for confession of sin or restitution, those steps should be taken, but hopelessly and continually moaning about the past or about missed opportunities will only blind us to today's opportunities and adventures. As we leave the past behind, our minds clear themselves of unwanted emotional baggage and open up for growth. However, if we try to live on the victories of yesterday or punish ourselves with its failures, we cannot expect success.

As a pastor, I've observed that many marital conflicts and career explosions came as a result of dwelling on failures remembered from old calendars. Fighting over history will never provide future peace. We must agree with Paul and say what he says: "I am forgetting the past—today!"

Paul also took a step of determination as he strained toward the future. You can almost feel the final push to the finish line. Paul's words appropriately belong in the successful man's spiritual Olympic time-trials. Remember, *you cannot give up and win.* By taking the winner's step of determination, we are sure of success if we forget the past and press on toward the future.

There's a third statement of determination that Paul lived. "I press toward the goal." Paul was committed to perseverance. He planned to reach his goal no matter what it took. You might be thinking to yourself, "I don't have the strength to keep pressing on!" But don't give up! Don't stop trying! Learn a lesson from two amphibians.

TWO FROGS IN CREAM

Two frogs fell into a can of cream,
    Or so I've heard it told;
The sides of the can were shiny and steep,
    The cream was deep and cold.
"O, what's the use?" croaked Number 1,
    'Tis fate; no help's around.
Goodbye, my friends! Goodbye, sad world!"
    And weeping still, he drowned.
But Number 2, of sterner stuff,
    Dogpaddled in surprise,
The while he wiped his creamy face
    And dried his creamy eyes.
"I'll swim awhile, at least," he said.
    Or so I've heard he said;
"It really wouldn't help the world
    If one more frog were dead."
An hour or so he kicked and swam,
    Not once he stopped to mutter,
But kicked and kicked and swam and kicked,
    Then hopped out, via butter!
        —*T.C. Hamlet*[1]

It's that kind of determination that will enable us to do things that some people only dream of accomplishing. Those who have been supercharged and electrified by the power of God's Spirit have an incredible advantage.

Then while you're walking, take a step of:

CONVICTION

Many have suffered tremendous ridicule and persecution because of their convictions...even in the secular world.

George Westinghouse was considered a lunatic by railroad executives. They said that "a man was crazy if he thought he could stop a train by wind." But Westinghouse finally sold the airbrake idea and became famous.

Charles Goodyear spent years in poverty, as well as prison, because of his debts. But one day he found the secret to vulcanizing rubber. Though he had labored for years on the idea, family and friends failed to see the worth of the discovery. But countless Goodyear stores honor his tenacity today as do four internationally visible blimps.

Wilbur Wilberforce became inflamed with the idea of stopping the slave trade and slavery in England. Goaded by Prime Minister Pitt, he spent years speaking against slavery and the slave trade, all the while suffering repeated defeats in Parliament. However, it was not until 1833 that Wilberforce learned, on his deathbed, that both houses of the Parliament finally abolished slavery in Britain.

Thomas Edison refused to give up when his first efforts to find an effective filament for the carbon incandescent lamp did not produce the desired results. On October 21, 1879, after thirteen months of repeated failures, he succeeded in his search for the proper filament. Continuing without sleep for over two days and nights, he finally managed to slip a carbonized cotton fiber into a vacuum sealed bulb and turned on the current. He declared, "The sight we had so long desired to see, finally met our eyes." His perseverance against discouraging odds gave lightbulbs to the world.

The Apostle Paul said:

All of us who are mature should take such a view of things. And if on some point you think differently, that too God will make clear to you. Only let us live up to what we have already attained. Join with others in following my example, brothers, and take note of those who live according to the pattern we gave you."

(Philippians 3:15-17)

Paul was confident of his God-given calling and divine directive for his words. He knew that if any disagreed with him, God would show them the truth. Paul knew the power of the Holy Spirit to cement conviction—conviction that would give a believer the strength to suffer, even die, for what he knew was right.

It is this type of conviction, *based upon the reality of God's Word,* that makes real winners out of God's people. After we determine to have God's best, He expects us to take a step of conviction. It is a bold, unswerving step, made with complete confidence.

What motivated Hezekiah and Nehemiah to work wholeheartedly for the Lord? What drove Paul, with great compassion and vigor, to seek God's will for his life, being satisfied with nothing less? The answer is simple: Each of God's winners have proper motivation. It's not an external motivation from family, friends, or pep squads. It's the internal force of the Holy Spirit driving us on to victory.

One Sunday night, a pastor asked members of the congregation to share their favorite Scripture verses. One little girl had just memorized John 3:16 and was excited about publicly reciting it. She stood and quoted: "For God so loved the world, that He gave His only begotten

Son, that whosoever believeth in Him, should not perish, but have *internal* life." No one dared to correct her. That's exactly what God does. He gives internal life as well as eternal life. Jesus said, "I have come that they may have life, and have it to the full" (John 10:10). The only way that we can ever have the right motivation to be a success in life is to experience God's *internal* life. It is the inward drive of God living in us, causing us to become more Christ-like and producing true success.

The story is told of a dog who boasted of his ability as a runner. One day he chased a rabbit but failed to catch his prey. The other dogs ridiculed him because of his boasting. "You must remember," he said to them in reply, "that the rabbit was running for his life, while I was only running for my dinner." The key determinant in what we win at is our internal incentive. To persevere in the pilgrimage to the top has always taken—and always will take—something special within. But for the believer, it's not a "something," but a "Someone"—Jesus Christ as Lord of our lives.

Notes:
[1] Taken from *Encyclopedia of 7,700 Illustrations: Signs of the Times* by Paul Lee Jan, ThD., Assurance Publishers. Used by permission.

Chapter 7/ It's Who You Know

The winners in the Old Testament believed that God's powerful presence was in their lives. It was a sure foundation for ultimate victory because they firmly believed, "If God be for us, who can stand against us?" For them, God spoke directly and gave them this promise:

"This is how you will know that the living God is among you...the ark of the covenant of the Lord of all the earth will go...ahead of you." (Joshua 3:11)

Only when they sought the Lord and followed Him did they have success in conquering their foes. The same is true for us today.

How do you know if God is in your life? Why is His presence in your life necessary in order to be a winner? Can you win on your own?

Never forget that winning involves a consistent lifestyle of being and doing everything that God wants for you. This characteristic is the icing on the winner's victory cake.

God Initiates Success

It was God who took the first step toward Joshua. Jehovah Himself initiated the conversation instructing His servant on the Israelites' future. Many years before Joshua's leadership, God spoke to Moses from a burning bush; then, many centuries later, to Paul from a blinding light.

At that moment at Pentecost when the Holy Spirit first indwelled believers, God started a revolutionary experience. I'm sure it was awe inspiring as Peter gave the first-humanly-exciting-but-heavenly-initiated invitation and saw thousands of people respond to Christ. The instant fellowship experienced in a local body of believers as praise is rendered; the pure heavenly electricity that surges through believers as they worship together today is equally exhilarating. God initiates that, too.

There is nothing positive that you can wholesomely enjoy that God has not given. Marriage, friendships, careers, recreation, hobbies, and most of all, salvation. We are to enjoy our personal, intimate relationship with the Lord of glory. Romans 5:8 says, "...God demonstrates His own love for us in this: While we were still sinners, Christ died for us." And in I Timothy 6:17 we see the marvelous assurance, "Command those who are rich in this present world not to be arrogant nor to put their hope in wealth, which is so uncertain, but to put their hope in God, *who richly provides us with everything for our enjoyment.* What a wonderful Lord!

God wants us to understand that He desires us to be successful in life—according to His definition and provision. He has already initiated it. Accept His invitation and go with *His* flow.

God Orders Success

The command for Joshua and his people was, "Get ready!" The promised success was about to become reality. Jehovah God ordered the people to prepare themselves spiritually for success. In doing so, they learned several things about God's orders that we need to know, too.

First, God's orders are never harmful. Many people believe that if they do what God wants them to do, He'll ruin their good time and send them to Africa as missionaries. But exactly the opposite is the case. When we don't follow His orders, misery is sure to follow—from our own hand. His orders are never harmful; He wants only the best for us because He created us and cares about us. And, if God does call you to Africa to be a missionary, it will be best for others, and for you as well! You'll not only want to go (remember the God-given desires of the heart?), you'll find in it true enjoyment.

Second, God's orders are never complex. God gives simple orders. He gave Joshua one phrase, "Get ready." It was an order a child could understand. God has also gone to great lengths to ensure that we understand His commands. The Old Testament laws were summed up in the Ten Commandments (Exodus 20) and repeated in the New Testament (Romans 13:9). These were simple, direct, easy-to-understand commands. The New Testament was written in Koine Greek, popular between 330 B.C. and 330 A.D. as the everyday language of everyday people. Though a complex language, its meanings were simple and exact in describing every imaginable action. He's preserved His Word and given it to us today for our good. It's still simple and clear, requiring our obedience.

Third, God's orders are always helpful. If God tells you, "No," it is only so He can later say, "Yes," to something better. He's on your side (Romans 8:31-38).

There are many concepts that we, who operate on a different plane than God, do not fully understand. We often run into a wall (sometimes labeled "failure") because we have not followed the One who opens the door. He expects us to obey His orders, confident that God knows what's best and is waiting to give it to us.

God declared success for Joshua and the children of Israel. He told them exactly what they would do, where they would go, and what they would be. Listen for His declarations for your life and, instead of swimming upstream, let yourself be carried to success in His current. Hundreds of godly pronouncements for our lives exist in the Word of God. All spell w-i-n-n-e-r, regardless of what the situation looks like now.

The heroes of the Bible were not spectacular, extraordinary individuals; they were common, everyday men and women with similar concerns to ours of today. Many, like Moses, had to be persuaded toward victory, because God desires people who are Savior-confident, rather than self-confident. Those who trust God to do what only He can do experience the fruit of heaven-inspired victory rather than ego-driven defeat.

God Motivates True Success

We cannot leave this passage without being brought face-to-face with how God motivates success. Look through Joshua 1:6-7 and you'll read one of the greatest pep talks the world has ever heard.

"Be strong and courageous, because you will lead these people to inherit the land I swore to their forefathers to give them. Be strong and very courageous. Be careful to obey all the law my servant Moses gave you; do not turn from it to the right or to the left, that you may be successful wherever you go."

Two times in two verses, God tells Joshua to be "strong and courageous." Then, in Joshua 1:9, He says again, *"Have I not commanded you? Be strong and courageous. Do not be terrified; do not be discouraged, for the Lord your God will be with you wherever you go."*

There were four sentences God said to encourage

Joshua. Look at those four repetitive phrases:
1. Be strong.
2. Be very courageous.
3. Do not be terrified.
4. Do not be discouraged.

Jehovah was saying three basic things to Joshua. First, He said, "Be strong," and then He encouraged His warrior with, "Do not be terrified." Put the two together: It wasn't going to be easy. But God was also telling His servant: Don't let fear drain your strength or trust in me. Be strong. . .and do not be terrified.

When fear enters our lives, strength and trust depart. God did not want that for Joshua, so He encouraged him to "Be strong." The absence of fear causes us to walk undaunted through the lion's den of today's world.

But God also told Joshua: "Be very courageous and do not be discouraged."

What happens to courage when the three little letters D-I-S precede it? Dis-couragement. The one precludes the other. God was telling Joshua to lead the very people who tried to kill Moses. Joshua probably needed some encouragement. He was an individual in the midst of great turmoil. On one hand, he was leading a people whose emotional state was very volatile, and on the other, he was leading them into a land filled with giants. A formidable situation! On the edge of the wilderness, camped by the Jordan River, God promised him, "You are going to take the entire area in front of you. It's yours." These people were escaped slaves. They had never had anything, so why should they think that they were going to have everything now? Encouragement from Jehovah was necessary for His people to enter the Promised Land victoriously. Without it, they would never even have tried!

The Lord's words became a well of encouragement to the personal, emotional thirst of Joshua. God promised that He would take care of him, regardless of the situation, and gave him clear directions for victory. That's the kind of assurance we desperately need to claim. As Christians, we are tempted to walk by sight instead of faith as we look at our world situation. We tend to look at what *we* can do physically or intellectually. That's why, if we want to be real winners, we must allow God to encourage us through His Word. Winners in the Bible and winners today know that God's presence and their complete obedience determine success.

There was another phrase that God wanted Joshua to hear: "As I was with Moses, so I will be with you." Today, He tells us, "I will never leave you or forsake you" (Hebrews 13:5).

Then, for additional reinforcement, Jehovah said, "For the Lord your God will be with you wherever you go." The Old Testament tells us over and over that those who wanted to be successful always sought to determine if God was on their side before they acted. It's a question we, too, need to ask before we act. "Am I on God's side?" If you have surrendered your life, your heart, your soul to Christ, giving Him control, you are more than a conqueror (Romans 8:31,37). The Apostle Paul said it appropriately: "To them God has chosen to make known among the Gentiles the glorious riches of this mystery, which is Christ in you, the hope of glory" (Colossians 1:27).

Joshua was only Moses' aide, his errand boy, when God chose him. Samuel was a child when God called Him. David was the youngest of Jesse's boys when God chose him to be king. Mary was only a teenager when God chose her to become the mother of the Messiah.

Then there was Peter, an adult, but rough, rugged, and impulsive. He was skilled only in fishing when Jesus called, "Follow me and I will make you fishers of men." Matthew was at his desk when Jesus walked into his tax office, looked him straight in the eye and said, "Come, follow me." Paul was on a rampage, muttering murderous threats against God's people, when Jesus said, "Get up and go!"

God often chooses the least likely individual to be His instrument. You might even be saying to yourself, "Now, that's me...least likely to succeed!" But Jesus speaks to you even as He did to the apostles with these encouraging words: "You did not choose me, but I chose you to go and bear fruit" (John 15:16).

The Bible clearly illustrates the "how" of this!

"And if the Spirit of him who raised Jesus from the dead is living in you, he who raised Christ from the dead will also give life to your mortal bodies through his Spirit, who lives in you." (Romans 8:11)

"...Christ lives in me." (Galatians 2:20)

"For to me, to live is Christ....If I am to go on living in the body, this will mean fruitful labor for me." (Philippians 1:21-22)

When we accept Jesus Christ as Savior, He never leaves. We have a strong and mighty general ready to fight for us as only One who has never tasted defeat can do. And, as if to remove any possible Satan-generated doubt, John records Christ's eloquent words:

"...You do not believe because you are not my sheep. My sheep listen to my voice; I know them, and they follow me. I give them eternal life, and they shall never perish; no one can snatch them out of my hand. My Father, who has given them to me, is greater than all; no one can snatch

them out of my Father's hand. I and the Father are one." (John 10:26-29)

Claim victory with the Apostle Paul as he writes, "In all these things, we are more than conquerors through Him who loved us. "For I am convinced that neither death nor life, neither angels nor demons, neither the present nor the future, nor any powers, neither height nor depth, nor anything else in all creation, will be able to separate us from the love of God that is in Christ Jesus our Lord" (Romans 8:35-39). Maybe you're confused by present-day concepts taught by today's success-sultans. Heed the Word of God. *Your success is guaranteed and has been since the day you accepted Christ as Savior. You were born again as a conqueror through Jesus Christ your Lord.* You have been equipped by the King of Kings, Lord of Lords, and the great I Am. You can't get more successful than that!

It has been said that no man has a monopoly on the Holy Spirit, but time has proven that the Holy Spirit has a monopoly on few men.

Does God have a monopoly on you?

Are you convinced of God's powerful presence in your life?

Chapter 8/
Failure Pays

> Peter replied, "Man, I don't know what you're talking about!" Just as he was speaking, the rooster crowed. The Lord turned and looked straight at Peter. Then Peter remembered the word the Lord had spoken to him: "Before the rooster crows today, you will disown me three times." And he went outside and wept bitterly."
> (Luke 22:60-62)

Peter's denial of Christ. It has echoed in hearts through the centuries. But we shouldn't be too hard on Peter—for who knows how we would have responded in the same situation? It has been has said that "a noble failure serves as faithfully as a distinguished success." Scripture validates that statement with the example of the big fisherman, a special man who believed God for everything. Though we see a losing moment in his life, we also see that overall, Peter was a winner.

Do you remember the story of Jesus walking on the water? Peter was the only disciple who asked to walk out to Him (Matthew 14:28-29). In spite of his fear and the storm around him, Peter believed Jesus was able to do anything, anytime, and in any place.

Then, who could ever forget that day when Jesus asked the disciples the question, "Who do you say I am?" It was the winner, Peter, who proclaimed boldly, "You are the Christ, the Son of the living God" (Matthew 16:15-16).

No other disciple among the twelve stood as boldly for

Christ as Peter. But he failed! The strongest disciple broke under pressure. He lost in the most critical area of the Christian walk, denying the Lord not once, but three different times. His life is an example of the winner who loses, but bounces back. There are several things that we can learn from his failure so that when we lose, just like Peter, we, too, can bounce back. Failure can be God's will for your life; it may not be His perfect will, but He sometimes allows it. Edward Everett Hale, author and Chaplain of the U.S. Senate in the early 1900s, said, "You and I must not complain if our plans break down when we have done our part. That probably means that the plans of the One who knows more than we do have succeeded."

God does allow failure and it is not necessarily as judgment for past sins. At one time or another, we all fail in our different relationships, our careers, and in our spiritual lives. Even though most failure is self-inflicted, God often uses failure to reshape the rough edges in our lives that do not look like Jesus. At other times, God allows failures in our life because He cannot get our attention any other way. When we are finally brought to our knees, we have no other option but to depend upon Him rather than on ourselves. Failure can become a mirror in our life that shows us our need of God and allows the image of Christ-likeness to appear.

It is encouraging to know that our God is the God of the second chance. He can redeem anything, including our failures. What He did for Peter, He can—and will—do for us.

Maybe that's where you are right now, seated in the chair of remorse, next to a man named Peter. Don't stay seated! Instead, lean on Peter's Lord. Before Peter's denial and failure, Jesus prayed:

"Simon, Simon, Satan has asked to sift you as wheat. But I have prayed for you, Simon, that your faith may not fail. And when you have turned back, strengthen your brothers." (Luke 22:31-32)

By investigating Peter's failure, we discover several encouraging principles.

Look closely; Jesus *did not pray* that Peter would not fail, but that his *faith* would not fail. Jesus was encouraging him when He said, "Simon, I have prayed that your faith will not fail." If Peter's faith had failed, he wouldn't have been so emotionally upset after his denial. We might experience a setback on the outside, but God does not want us to fail on the inside. . .where it counts.

If Jesus prayed for Peter, knowing that in just a few short hours Peter would deny Him three times, we can know with certainty that Jesus is behind us, too. Many times we judge ourselves expecting God to join our "Woe is me!" chorus, but He never will. Did you notice that Jesus never condemned Peter for denying Him? Not once did Jesus ever say, "Peter, I'm so ashamed of you."

Then, one day a woman was caught in the act of adultery (John 8:1-11). They let the man get away, but a group of super-spiritual pseudo-saints threw the woman at the feet of Jesus. They said, "Jesus, the Law says this woman ought to be stoned for adultery. What do you say?" He only listened at first, silently writing in the sand; then He replied, "If any one of you is without sin, let him be the first to throw a stone at her." Slowly her accusers slunk away. And there she was, alone with the Savior, probably humiliated and still terrified. It's one thing to commit adultery, but another thing altogether to be caught in it. Public failure is always worse than private failure. Finally, Jesus said, "Where are your accusers?

Has no one condemned you?" Responding, "No, Sir," she looked into the eyes of One who knew no sin, Jesus Christ the Son of God. Then she heard a statement that set her free: "Then neither do I condemn you. Go now and leave your life of sin."

God supports us even in the midst of failure. In the depths of your defeats, remember that He is praying for you. Paul wrote, "In the same way, the Spirit helps us in our weakness. We do not know what we ought to pray, but the Spirit helps us in our weakness. We do not know what we ought to pray, but the Spirit himself intercedes for us with groans that words cannot express. And he who searches our hearts knows the mind of the Spirit, because the Spirit intercedes for the saints in accordance with God's will" (Romans 8:26-27). When self-condemnation strikes and you're teetering on the brink, hold on to that truth. Discover freedom from self-condemnation.

Many people seem to have the idea that God is "out to get them." They have lost sight of their infinite value in His eyes. If only we would accept God's heavenly perspective of what is occurring in our lives right now! Hebrews 12:1 offers tremendous encouragement to anyone who has failed:

"Therefore, since we are surrounded by such a great cloud of witnesses, let us throw off everything that hinders and the sin that so easily entangles, and let us run with perseverance the race marked out for us."

Imagine hosts of saints and millions of angels gathered around the throne of God intently watching your life. It's almost like a giant stadium of heavenly cheerleaders urging those who know Jesus to "Go! Go! Go!" They recognize no failure—only our commitment to the Lord and to "do better next time." "Because he himself suffered when he was tempted, he is able to help those who are being tempted" (Hebrews 2:18). "The Lord is faithful, and he will strengthen and protect you from the evil one" (II Thessalonians 3:3).

We find ourselves losing when we live our relationships and careers apart from God and His heavenly cheering section. God is for us, not against us. He wants us to win.

One reason that Jesus told Peter that He had prayed for him was that He knew Simon Peter would need to know it later. In those tragic moments of great bitterness, weeping, and repentance, I imagine he remembered the words of Christ: "Peter, I am praying for you that you will not lose your faith."

Jesus also knew that Peter was going to rise from the pits of failure to the heights of victory. The big fisherman was destined to become an achiever once again, and his failure would become a source of encouragement to millions because God would use it as a foundation for Peter's later success...and as encouragement to every other believer from then to now.

So, you've failed! Admit it. Acknowledge any personal sin, and listen to your heavenly cheering section urging you to "press on!" Your goal has not crashed and burned—you have —temporarily. Like Peter, keep following the Lord. Don't give up, especially on yourself! Peter's faith seemed to shatter into a thousand pieces when he failed in the one area in which he so desperately desired to succeed. But, he never stopped following his Lord.

Allow God to place in your heart that dream which He wants you to follow. The Bible teaches that He is our life (Colossians 3:3). Give Him first priority in your life, and He will create godly desires in your heart. Only then will your dreams come true—but you must keep following them with a passionate heart.

If you bounce back from failure, it will come as a result of following the dream put inside your heart by our heavenly Father. Don't stop to dwell on your failure as Peter did. Keep following that God-given dream regardless of how impossible it may seem.

Admittedly, sometimes it is hard to forget failure. So, when its haunting memory comes to your mind, take responsibility for your actions and your thoughts. Find the strength to fight off those destructive memories inside the fortress of the name of Jesus Christ. Proverbs 18:10 tells us, "The name of the Lord is a strong tower; the righteous run to it and are safe." It only compounds the problem if we blame our failures or their consequences on someone else or allow them a resting place in our minds.

When you fail, take responsibility for it. Peter accepted responsibility for his own actions, repented of his sin, and renewed his fellowship with God. If your failure is caused by personal sin, confess it to God (I John 1:9). Take your burden of sin to the Lord, and leave it there. If you do, He'll renew your spirit. We lose nothing but our agony and remorse when we turn to Him in repentance. If it was caused by poor judgment, unforeseen circumstances, natural disaster, or the machinations of others, remember that God is still in control. He is sovereign...and real faith means trusting and persevering even when we don't understand (Hebrews 11). But mere forgiveness and confident trust is not enough; constant fellowship with the Master is clearly prescribed.

It was early morning when the women went to anoint the body of Jesus following His crucifixion. Upon reaching the tomb, they found it empty except for the grave clothes, neatly folded. Then they saw Him—the risen Lord in His resurrected form. Immediately, they ran back to tell the apostles what had happened.

"It was Mary Magdalene, Joanna, Mary the mother of James, and the others with them who told this to the apostles. But they did not believe the women, because their words seemed to them like nonsense. Peter, however, got up and ran to the tomb." (Luke 24:10)

Did you catch that? After his greatest failure, instead of running *from* the Lord, Peter ran to *seek* the Lord. The lost fellowship was to be reclaimed! Instead of waiting for the Lord to look him up, he eagerly sought to initiate his return to the Lord. He and John were the only two disciples who sought the Lord. Everyone else sat around feeling sorry for themselves, mourning the last three-and-a-half years as wasted time. But not Peter! He craved the renewal of the intimate fellowship that he had once had with Christ. He probably thought, "If there's a chance that I can see Him, I've got to take it! I've got to get back to Him!"

During the forty days following the resurrection, Jesus appeared to different individuals in His glorified body. One morning, after fishing all night, the disciples neared the shore and saw a man making breakfast. As they came closer, one of the disciples cried, "It is the Lord!" Guess what happened? Peter jumped out of the boat and swam to Jesus. He couldn't wait for the boat to dock—he had to get to Jesus, even if he had to get wet! (John 21:4-7). When you fail and the dreams in your life seem to fall apart, do you run to—or from—the One who can bring them back to life—the risen Lord?

Then, train yourself to look positively at what has occurred in your life. Failure can become a dead weight or wings to fly. In every defeat, there is a positive perspective. Redeem your ruin. That mindset is one of the characteristics of real winners. The very thing in which we are the weakest can become our greatest strength if we will allow the Lord to redeem it and us. Peter learned that his desire to speak publicly for Christ was inadequate until he turned his words and boldness over to the Lord. Then he was transformed and his biggest area of weakness (his mouth!) became his greatest area of victory as recorded in Acts 2. Think of it. This same man who once publicly denied Christ before a slave girl was later emboldened by the Savior to publicly proclaim Him before thousands at Pentecost.

Peter also learned that he should first get God-given directions instead of going off inspired only with good intentions. Have you ever tried to assemble a seemingly simplistic toy without reading the instructions? You simply allow your mechanical prowess (or lack of!) to guide you. However, finishing through sheer determination, you find two or three key pieces left over. Several options are available: You can give in to frustration and stuff the toy in a closet; you can throw away those "significant pieces," or you can set aside *your* knowledge and start over with the directions. Peter was wise the second time around. As he returned to his power source, Jesus gave him two instructions: "Feed my sheep" and "wait in Jerusalem." This time, instead of taking off in his own strength, Peter followed the directions.

Don't let failure keep you pinned to the floor. You can bounce back regardless of how hard the fall. No matter how deep the wounds, defeat is only temporary if we get prompt spiritual aid. The Lord will provide mental, emotional, and spiritual healing if we seek His help.

Henry Ford once said, "Failure is only the opportunity to begin again, but more intelligently." Lord Kelvin, quoted in *Moody Monthly*[1], said "When you are face to face with a difficulty, you are up against a discovery."

Paul Harvey said, "Someday, I hope to enjoy enough of what the world calls success so that if somebody asks me, 'What's the secret of it?' I shall say this: 'I get up when I fall down.' "

Get up. Stand up. Get ready to fly again. Regardless of how, where, or when we fail—and you can depend on the certainty that at some point you *will* fail at something—we can bounce back. Oh yes, winners lose, but real winners never quit. Victory is part of the believer's heritage.

Notes:
[1] Taken from *Knight's Master Book of New Illustrations,* compiled by Walter B. Knight © 1956, reprinted in 1986, p. 470, William B. Erdmans Publishing Co., Grand Rapids, Michigan. Used with permission.

Chapter 9/ Powerful Principles

> Now Israel loved Joseph more than any of his other sons, because he had been born to him in his old age; and he made a richly ornamented robe for him. When his brothers saw that their father loved him more than any of them, they hated him and could not speak a kind word to him. (Genesis 37:3-4)
>
> The Lord was with him; he showed him kindness and granted him favor in the eyes of the prison warden. So the warden put Joseph in charge of all those held in the prison, and he was made responsible for all that was done there. The warden paid no attention to anything under Joseph's care, because the Lord was with Joseph and gave him success in whatever he did. (Genesis 39:21-23)
>
> So Pharaoh asked them, "Can we find anyone like this man, one in whom is the spirit of God?" Then Pharaoh said to Joseph, "Since God has made all this known to you, there is no one so discerning and wise as you. You shall be in charge of my palace, and all my people are to submit to your orders. Only with respect to the throne will I be greater than you. (Genesis 41:38-40)

Have you ever found yourself in a situation where everything in your life has come apart? Nothing is going right. Failure haunts your every decision, and the only way out is up because you have already hit the bottom. There's strife in the family. Your career is about to change because the market or company has shifted and your services are no longer required. You can't get a loan from the bank. You're so broke you can't even pay attention! To make matters worse, you go to your car and find a flat tire, a dead battery, and no credit cards. Even your instant money card is "eaten" by the computerized teller machine. It seems that the walls of life are crumbling around you and the foundation on which you stand feels like it is in a California earthquake! The only help you're getting is from friends who talk from a comfortable, secure, announcer's booth, giving an unrequested commentary on your life.

Sound familiar? There are many people who run from their present situations looking for a new one: a new family, a new wife (or husband), a new career, or a new location. They have one objective: get out of the current circumstance and start over. Believing that it is easier to run, they turn into jumpers, bailing out—most often without a parachute. Usually, though, this strategy leads only from one losing situation to another.

Have you seen the picture of the little kitten hanging on to a limb, suspended over unknown dangers? Captioned beneath the scene are the words: "Hang in there!" Maybe you feel like that little kitty right now. If so, "hang in there." The issue is still survival.

Let's take a look at the life of Joseph. Joseph's life was certainly not a bowl of cherries, but his lifestyle reveals ten principles to being a winner in losing situations.

At the age of seventeen, Joseph, the youngest son of Jacob, is a favored child. However, his father's favoritism caused tremendous resentment in the hearts of his brothers, eventually stirring up hatred at home. Added to this were the prophetic dreams and interpretations that God had given Joseph concerning his future. Not being shy or humble, Joseph informed his family that they would one day be his servants. Needless to say, Joseph became a real source of irritation to his brothers. Their jealousy and distaste for him grew into a plot to take his life. However, Reuben and Judah intervened, and Joseph was sold by his brothers to Midianite merchants, who in turn sold him as a slave to an Egyptian. His famous coat of many colors, which his father had made for him, was sprinkled with blood and ripped to shreds to cover up the despicable brotherly betrayal. The lie about his son's death from the would-be assassins caused Jacob to mourn for nearly two decades and to live with his grief over the lad's death.

Meanwhile, Joseph was sold as a slave to Potiphar, one of Pharaoh's officers and captain of the guards. The Bible reveals that Joseph was successful even as a slave because God was with him. He so impressed Potiphar with his administrative skills that he was put in charge of the entire household. Joseph's losing situation turned into a winning situation—except for one small detail, Mrs. Potiphar. Hungry for attention and affection, this Egyptian housewife began to "put the moves" on the young Hebrew. He resisted her seduction and maintained his purity, but lost his cloak while literally running away from her.

Mrs. Potiphar didn't like being rejected. False accusations against Joseph were presented to Captain Potiphar. For a second time, Joseph became the object of wrath and a victim of unjust circumstances. He was thrown into prison because he had done the right thing. Think of how it must have felt for this young man. He had hit the bottom of life, falling from favored son to slave to convict.

Joseph was not climbing the ladder of success; rather, he was sliding rapidly down the chute of failure. But even in an Egyptian prison, he found favor in the warden's eye because of his noticeable, God-given administrative skills which he used faithfully even in an unjust situation. Over a period of time he was promoted to Head Trustee and given responsibility to direct the entire prison.

Then, as God, who was still in control, had it planned, the cupbearer and the baker from Pharaoh's court displeased Pharaoh and were thrown into Joseph's domain. While sleeping one night, these men had alarming dreams. Joseph, sensitive to their needs, interpreted their dreams for them. For one man, the interpretation meant death, but for the other, restoration to his former job. Joseph asked the cupbearer to remember him when he returned to his position in Pharaoh's court. . . .But the cupbearer forgot. For two more years, Joseph remained in an Egyptian dungeon.

Then it happened! Pharaoh had two dreams that no one could interpret. Finally, the cupbearer remembered his experience with Joseph and recommended his services to his royal Egyptian employer. Joseph interpreted the dreams and impressed Pharaoh. So much so that the king asked, "Can we find anyone like this man, one in whom is the spirit of God?" Even Pharaoh recognized the source of Joseph's wisdom and gifts and elevated Joseph from the prison to the palace, making him second only to Pharaoh, the greatest power-broker of the world.

During the famine that Joseph foresaw in the dreams, his family came to Egypt and sought his help. The story has a happy ending, with the family united in fellowship and love in Egypt, but the path to it was not an easy one.

If any man had his share of both losing and winning, it was Joseph. Count them. Joseph had three different, major setbacks, but he became a winner in each one. If you ever find yourself in a losing situation, practice Joseph's principles and become a winner.

Principle 1: Live One Day At A Time

You never find Joseph worrying about tomorrow or complaining about yesterday's spilt milk. Scripture never indicates that to be the pattern or attitude of his life. Not once do we see him sitting in the dungeon or in Potiphar's home wringing his hands over tomorrow or perspiring with fear for his life. Questions like, "How can I get back to my homeland and what am I going to do tomorrow?" were never uttered. He accepted and lived a day at a time. Joseph passed every stress test the world gave him. Do you?

Anxious moments occur because we try to live more than one day at a time. Just as it is physically impossible to do so, it is also emotionally impossible. Jesus said, "Do not worry about tomorrow, for tomorrow will worry about itself. Each day has enough trouble of its own" (Matthew 6:34). Live only *one day at a time*. The stress of trying to worry about tomorrow is too great—and not Christ honoring. If we believe God is in control, we must act like it. The Lord only gives us one moment at a time to enjoy. "Therefore do not worry about tomorrow, for tomorrow will worry about itself" (Matthew 6:34). We're not promised a tomorrow, so why should we worry about it before it comes? "Cast all your anxiety on him because he cares for you" (I Peter 5:7). It's a command God expects us to obey.

Principle 2: Make The Most Out Of The Bad

Joseph threw no boo-hoo-banquets, no pity parties. While he was in Potiphar's household, he decided he would do his best and be the best slave possible. Looking at his situation from a positive perspective, he refused to moan or whine about the terrible injustice or that he didn't deserve to be treated like this. In prison, he committed himself to be the epitome of a faithful, honest prisoner. That's a tough prescription to fill!

During my first pastorate, one summer Sunday night I encouraged our church family to think the best about bad situations. "Always find the positive in the midst of negative situations," I preached. Finally I asked, "Does anybody have a positive perspective of a bad situation?" One lady, without any hesitation, got up and said, "I would just like to praise the Lord for my broken toilet." The silence was broken as she continued, "Our toilet literally came apart and ruined the entire bathroom. But, I just want to praise the Lord because now I'm going to have the opportunity to redecorate that ugly bathroom. I've hated it ever since we moved into that house." Her humor and transparency encouraged others.

God uses those bad situations to fine-tune the gifts that He has given us, to prepare us for what's ahead. So, instead of looking at a losing situation as another "cross to bear," view it as a practice session to sharpen your skills of emotional and spiritual development.

It might be through that tough situation in your life that God opens up a brand new area of opportunity. Had Joseph not gone through those difficult years, he might not have ended up as Vice-Pharaoh. In each of those potentially devastating situations, Joseph remained a godly man in God's place. It may only be after the storms of life that God reveals the rainbow for you. Will you be as faithful as Joseph in your tough times?

The story is told of a young preacher who had given up hope in his first pastorate. He went to a convention and saw a famous preacher, the pastor of a very large and influential church. Approaching him, he said, "Sir, I am very unhappy where I am serving. I just can't get people to follow me. They don't seem to listen. If, in your travels, you come across another church who is looking for a pastor and you feel led, would you consider passing my name along?" Expecting a "Yes, sir, I will" answer, he was stunned when the preacher said, "Listen, young man, I'm going to tell you something. Don't you ever forget this. You'll never be happy anywhere until you get happy where you are."

Life is filled with all kinds of tough situations and problems. "Pull a Joseph" in the midst of them. Make the best out of each negative situation and get happy where you are!

Principle 3: Keep Pure

Youthful and handsome. That was Joseph, Captain Potiphar's head slave. You can imagine the sexual pressure placed upon this young man by the lonesome, attractive "military widow." Mrs. Potiphar had her sights upon the young Hebrew. She began a siege against his soul and a powerful claim for his body. Declaring that he would never sin against his heavenly or earthly master, Joseph resisted, and he paid a high price for his purity. No one can tell you that by living a pure life, you're going to be free from problems. In fact, like Joseph, your purity may even *cause* problems. But, if you do have to pay a price for purity, always remember who you are really honoring by your stand—God. Trust Him to take your situation and transform it, just as He did for Joseph.

Keep pure, but stay alert. When we begin to grow in the Lord, seeking an unblemished lifestyle, Satan will throw everything he can at us, including the kitchen sink of temptation. Keep alert. "Your enemy the devil prowls around like a roaring lion looking for someone to devour" (I Peter 5:8). Don't be that someone!

If ever you need a direct line to heaven, it's when you're in a losing situation. Sin breaks our fellowship with God and hinders our prayers (James 5:16). Stay in touch with the Father in the midst of any problem so you can hear His voice clearly.

Joseph's life reveals that whatever price we pay for rejecting sin and temptation, *it is worth it.* All the success in the world can never buy a clean mind washed by a pure life.

Principle 4: Do What You Do Well

As we follow Joseph's example, there is a silver thread that can be observed in his life. He did whatever he did well, regardless of his situation. Administration was his one glowing talent that all the world could see and admire. In each bad situation, he just kept on doing what he knew he could do—administrate!

Be consistent in doing what you do very well. Remember, when problems occur in your life, it *may not* be that God is saying that you need to change occupations or directions. God expects us to be faithful stewards of the talents and abilities He has given us. It's one way we give honor to Him. And on the other side of that issue, we must not assume we can do everything. God expects us to listen to the leading of the Holy Spirit, then obey, whether it means staying in or leaving a difficult situation. We can choose to respond to the days of preparation positively, by waiting patiently and prayerfully for God to show us His ending to the turmoil.

Joseph proved that he could be trusted to do the menial things as well as the important ones. However, he never had the opportunity to do the "big thing" until he had proved himself diligent in the difficult things. Eventually, God *did* make him faithful over much. But Joseph had already decided that whatever happened, fame or futility, he would do what he could do, the best that he could do it. His life is an incredible encouragement for us. Regardless of how unpleasant our working conditions, or how unappreciated we feel, we must give it our best, our godly best. Each situation is an opportunity to improve our skills, stretching for the peak of perfection. Our circumstances may change, but our consistency in doing what we do well will be like a full moon on a dark night. We will light up the night for others. . .and for ourselves.

Principle 5: Be Sensitive To Others

Joseph had managerial skills just waiting to be used, but he had even a greater gift: sensitivity. Something very interesting occurs in Genesis 40 as the cupbearer and baker pour out their anguished hearts to him.

When Joseph came to them the next morning, he saw that they were dejected. So he asked Pharaoh's officials who were in custody with him in his master's house, "Why are your faces so sad today?" "We both had dreams," they answered, "but there is no one to interpret them." Then Joseph said to them, "Do not interpretations belong to God? Tell me your dreams." (Genesis 40:6-8)

When he could have been thinking about himself,

complaining about his unjust sentence, or planning how to escape the prison, he was involved with other people's problems. He had enough trouble himself, much less taking on anyone else's. But it was these seemingly insignificant, hurting people in his life who turned out to be the individuals God would use to catapult him to unbelievable success.

So what about us? Are we sensitive to those around us who hurt, regardless of who they are? Instead of saying, "Woe is me," we need to look to hurting, hungry people. Not for the sake of future favors, but because of our position. If we know Christ as Savior, we are children of the King in whom God has put His redemptive nature. It was because Joseph was sensitive to the needs of others, even in prison, that his life took a U-turn. Joseph's cell mates "looked dejected." Have you ever seen a happy prisoner? I'm sure Joseph saw many emotional wrecks, but these men must have looked *really* despondent. Joseph said, "Tell me all about it." He interpreted their dreams, and they came true. But two more miserable, lonely years passed in which Joseph probably felt rejected, forgotten, maybe even hopeless. Our lives may run similar paths with unexpected individuals opening up doors of success. But whether it happens or not, when we're in a losing situation, we have to keep our eyes on the Lord, then on others—not on ourselves. Focusing on other hurting people prevents self-absorption in our own problems.

Principle 6: Wait For God's Timing

Waiting is the hardest thing to do...at any age. Do you ever pray, "Lord, please give me patience...now!"? The United States Olympic team's motto is "swifter, higher,

stronger," but few know the Christian's Olympic motto: *Be still before the Lord and wait patiently for him; do not fret when men succeed in their ways, when they carry out their wicked schemes." (Psalm 37:7)
Why?
Those who hope in the Lord will renew their strength. They will soar on wings like eagles; they will run and not grow weary, they will walk and not be faint. (Isaiah 40:31)

Those words offer a wonderful promise, although they are tough to practice. Joseph had to wait until the Father opened the right doors at the right time. So do we. An old Italian proverb says that, "God never shuts a door without opening a window." Do you feel like there are doors slamming shut in your life? Wait for the window that God opens. It will be the perfect one to lead you to success...even if it only opens on to the fire escape.

Let's face it, nothing is more frustrating than to put ourselves on God's timetable. Often we cry out, "I don't have time to wait;" but when we run ahead of God, we get into trouble. Abraham's life is a good lesson for us. God promised Abraham and Sarah a child (Genesis 15:4). Instead of waiting for God's timing, though, they used human reasoning and Hagar, Sarah's handmaiden, to produce a child. Her son, Ishmael, and the promised son of Abraham and Sarah, Isaac, have been at war ever since. Two people, both God's people, ran ahead of God's timing.

We can also learn from the Hebrew hero, Moses. In Numbers 20:8, he was told to speak to the rock and drinking water would come forth. Instead, in anger or vexation with the people, he struck the boulder. Water gushed forth, but God said, "Moses, you're over eighty years old, and you still haven't learned to trust me.

Because of your disobedience, you will not go into the promised land" (20:12; 27:12-14). If only we could learn the skill of waiting some other way than by just waiting!

It's all right to wonder what's going on in your life. But as you try to figure out what God is planning, wait patiently for His perfect timing. It's simply a matter of trust.

Principle 7: Give God Glory

To be a winner in a losing situation, we must give credit where credit is due. *Give God the glory and honor.* Remember Joseph? He was finally called upon to interpret Pharaoh's dreams. This was his big chance! Think of it...for thirteen long years Joseph had been in bondage, facing one losing situation after another. It was the interpretation of dreams that got him into trouble in the first place, and now, it was going to be the same gift that would skyrocket him to success. But at a time when he could have taken personal credit for dream interpretation, he didn't. Observe how a man who had learned to be a winner even in seemingly losing situations answered the most powerful man in the world:

Pharaoh said to Joseph, "I had a dream, and no one can interpret it. But I have heard it said of you that when you hear a dream you can interpret it." (Genesis 41:15)

See the temptation that was before him? Joseph had the opportunity to make himself sound really important. Remember where Joseph had been and how long he had waited for this wonderful opportunity. But he passed up his "big chance" to upstage God. "I cannot do it," Joseph replied to Pharaoh, "but God will give Pharaoh the answer he desires" (Genesis 41:16).

What a godly man! In a moment symbolic of a life of self-denial and God-dependence, he said, "I can't do it, but God can." Many times the greatest temptation we will face will be the decision to glorify God in the midst of triumph—or to take personal credit. It's easy to trust God when things are rough because there's no one else to depend on. But it's another thing altogether to give God the glory when you're about to reach your personal peak of achievement. We can see that Joseph had walked with Jehovah for many years; he didn't forget Him. Notice that through it all—family rejection, slavery, and prison—Joseph's faith in the promises of God apparently never wavered. Not once did he even try to usurp the praise that belonged to Jehovah God.

Many years ago in a concert in Chicago, Harry Lauder, Scottish singer and songwriter, sang to a packed house. At the conclusion, the audience stood, *en masse*. The applause shook the entire house. As it died down, the audience began to cry, "Thank you! Thank you!" With great humility, Lauder responded, "Don't thank me. Thank the good Lord, who put the songs in my heart." It stands as a challenge to us: Give God the credit in our trials and in our triumphs.

Principle 8: Maintain A Forgiving Spirit

Sometimes we find ourselves in a losing situation due to our own misplaced priorities or outright blunders. If this is true, we need to forgive ourselves, although it's easier said than done. Sometimes, though, we are catapulted into the furnace by a fellow Christian. It's in this type of painful situation that real healing must take place.

In Genesis 42, it has been twenty years since Joseph saw

those conniving brothers who sold him into bondage. His brothers, his own family, had hated him that much! From the pit he had probably heard them discussing what they were going to do with him. One of the reasons he may not have been overly anxious about leaving Egypt was because he was afraid for his life. They had tried to kill him once; they might try again. But something had occurred in Israel that humbles the hardest of men—a famine. With all their grain resources depleted, his brothers came to him, via Pharaoh, asking for help. However, Joseph's reply did not come from a human spirit, but, rather, from a heavenly one:

> *Then Joseph said to his brothers, "Come close to me." When they had done so, he said, "I am your brother Joseph, the one you sold into Egypt! And now, do not be distressed and do not be angry with yourselves for selling me here, because it was to save lives that God sent me ahead of you. For two years now, there has been famine in the land, and for the next five years there will not be plowing and reaping. But God sent me ahead of you to preserve for you a remnant on earth and to save your lives by a great deliverance. So then, it was not you who sent me here, but God. He made me father to Pharaoh, lord of his entire household and ruler of Egypt."* (Genesis 45:4-8)

Imagine the fear that swept through the hearts of the brothers who had once betrayed him. But, Joseph had walked closely with the Lord through twenty difficult years. God had fashioned in him a forgiving spirit and a divine insight that showed him God's purpose.

It's hard to forgive people, especially those who wrong you. Many times I hear people say, "I can forgive so-and-so, but I just can't forget." The problem is, we can't forgive without forgetting! The Bible says that God forgives our sin, separating it from us as far as the east is from the west (Psalm 103:12). The human response is, "Well, that's God. That's not me!" But, the more Christ-like we are (or become), the more forgiveness will become our response also. But the more hate we harbor, the more destruction occurs inside us. Hate is the most virulent cancer of the spirit we can willfully choose to harbor. It also takes the joy from our Christian life, ruining our walk with Christ. It creates a bondage, a prison of personal sin, that is ours until we repent and ask forgiveness for an unforgiving spirit, relinquishing the "rights" that were violated.

Personally, I like the little boy's definition of forgiveness that says, "Forgiveness is the fragrance that flowers breathe when they're trampled on." That's exactly what forgiveness is! It's a heavenly fragrance that only God can give His people, who are rooted in Him, when they are trampled on by the world and others.

Ralph Waldo Emerson once said of Abraham Lincoln: "His heart is as great as the world, but there is no room in it for the memory of wrong." The great pulpiteer and pastor, Charles Hadden Spurgeon encouraged, "Cultivate a crop of forbearance in your life and pray that it yields a great harvest. Then, pray for a short memory as to unkindness."

Martin Niemoller was held many months in one of Hitler's prisons. He finally emerged from that experience saying, "It took me years to understand and realize that God is not the enemy of His enemies." Since God is like that, and if He lives inside our lives, then we can be like that, too. How? By consciously allowing the Spirit of God to produce in us the beautiful fragrance of forgiveness. As we do, we'll see the bloom of forgetfulness in our lives as well.

Principle 9: Take The Long Look

As Joseph spoke to his brothers, we get a long look at his entire life. Stop and think for a moment. As you pass through tough situations in your life, do you dwell on distasteful past situations? In order to be a winner in distasteful situations, we must take the long redemptive look at the past through the filter of God's perspective.

Joseph knew that if all that had happened had not taken place, he would not have been in a position to help his family when they needed it most. In fact, his position in Egypt meant the very survival of the Messianic people. Joseph's "long look" allowed him to visualize—humbly—his destiny and place in history. His "long look" assured him that God was in charge of his circumstances even though they were unfavorable and he was in a foreign land.

When things go bad and your situations become unbearable, take the long look. Regardless of how dark your night, it will soon be daybreak. Don't let a few hours of fear rob you of the bright days ahead.

Principle 10: Establish The Right Relationship

The most important thing that Joseph ever did was the foundation that sustained him through each unbearable situation. Joseph had a personal, active relationship with God. It was only by God's strength and presence that Joseph was able to take every bad thing that the world dished out to him. Because of his relationship with God, he became a winner. Joseph was not a politician, and he was anything but an "apple polisher." He knew that his personal priority had to be with the Father because God was in control of his destiny. Though he didn't know what tomorrow held, and he probably didn't like many of his todays, he knew beyond a shadow of a doubt who held tomorrow. That relationship was more valuable to him than all the wealth in Pharaoh's treasury.

To be a winner in a losing situation, we must have a right relationship with God. How do we develop and maintain such a relationship?

I was awakened one morning by a tender, little voice. It was our two-year-old son who had slipped into our bed well before the adult waking hours. "Dad-dy, Dad-dy," called the cherub faced munchkin. Hoping that my wife would answer the call, I peeked toward her side of the bed only to see her pillow over her head and ears. Then it came again, splitting the silence, "Dad-dy, Dad-dy!" Turning over on my left side, our eyes met—I was caught! "Hi!" came the swift introduction to a new day. It was time to get up, get moving, and start a brand-new week. However, before I could move a muscle, a new phrase came from our youngest, "Daddy, *me eat!*" The first order of the day: ME EAT! Constant consumption of mass quantities of food is his present goal in life. Waking hungry and staying hungry, that's our son. ME EAT! Then it hit me! How much more should we, as believers in the Lord Jesus Christ and children of God the Father, awake and remain hungry. Hungry for His presence! Hungry for His direction! Hungry for His Word! Hungry for prayer!

Oh, Father, make us all like my son, entering your presence with one plea: ME EAT!

That's what a right relationship with God is all about.

A right relationship with God is not just personal, it is also noticed publicly by others. Even the pagan Pharaoh noticed it!

> *So Pharaoh asked them, "Can we find anyone like this man, one in whom is the spirit of God?" Then Pharaoh said to Joseph, "Since God has made all this known to you, there is no one so discerning and wise as you."* (Genesis 41:38-39)

Losing situations? Life is filled with them! But winners are those in whom the Spirit and wisdom of God can be seen. Can it be seen in you?

Chapter 10/
Interrupted Plans

Sometimes life is a puzzle. When we are young and ambitious, we dream and search for greatness in our lives and careers. Whether they be high and lofty or practical and realistic, we never want to stay where we are, but to advance. Prosperity—in whatever terms we define it—is our ultimate goal.

But what do you do when things don't go like the plan? What do you do when your aspirations vanish like the early morning fog? Nothing feels more frustrating than for the direction of our plans to be changed. A sense of desperation seeps into our emotional makeup, often filling us with emptiness. Shattered dreams and broken hopes cause unspeakable despair.

If you have lost a dream, the story of John the Baptist should encourage your heart when things don't go like your plans. Four things surface in John's life that help us see what to do when things don't go as planned.

The Disruption That Occurs

John the Baptist was a successful, fiery prophet, but his career took a turn for the worse. It was not John's habit to soften the truth for any man. As he spoke out against wrong, his own physical safety was jeopardized.

Herod Antipas had visited his brother in Rome where he seduced his brother's wife. After dismissing his own wife, he married his sister-in-law. John the Baptist began to speak out against Herod publicly and sternly (Mark 6:14-29). However, it was never safe to rebuke an eastern despot. Herod's revenge led swiftly to the incarceration of the prophet. In the dungeons of the Machaerus Fortress, John the Baptist saw his plan disrupted. And what a disruption! For any man, dungeon life would have been a terrible fate, but for John, a child of the desert, it must have been even worse. All his life, he had lived in wide open spaces with the wind for walls and the sky for a roof. Now, he was confined within the four narrow walls of a filthy, dark dungeon. Physically limited, he could not accomplish what he saw as the plan for his life. For the first time, he was not in control of his day's activities. Socially limited, his only contacts were with other prisoners, or through the barred walls with followers who had become his disciples over the years. No longer could he stand in freedom and preach repentance. He was physically and emotionally trapped, completely hindered from doing what he was called to do.

How often have we found ourselves in the very same place as John the Baptist? A disruption has occurred in our lives. It may not be as harsh, but it's just as devastating. The things that we had planned have not turned out as envisioned. We find ourselves watching the parade of success detour around our street.

Perhaps a broken marriage has torn the dream of a wonderful, Christian home from your heart. Anxiety has replaced joy; frustration has replaced commitment. Perhaps a job has fallen through and the roots of your life have been ripped from under you like a tree uprooted in a violent storm. Do you feel as though life has turned a chainsaw loose on you? Are you torn by the gusts of adversity as the financial banner of your life flies tattered in the wind? Tomorrow is uncertain and today, at its best, is unstable.

Fear? We learn the meaning of the word early in life. The dream of "honor roll" students doesn't come to pass. Failures on their part darken the rainbow skies of expectation. Possibly, parents relive their own misspent youth through the catastrophes in their children's lives. Maybe a move to a new town has not produced the prospects promised. Crushed hopes, wounded egos, and disillusionment have crept into your life.

You, me, and John the Baptist have much in common. Even in that dungeon, he held all the aspirations of a great ministry that would usher in the kingdom of God, but he found himself filled with discouragement and disappointment.

Perhaps you feel condemned at this point in your pilgrimage. Just beyond your reach, you see fruit you cannot grasp. To make matters worse, there are:

The Doubts That Surface

Like John the Baptist, we may find doubts surfacing.

Remember that John baptized Jesus. He even saw the Holy Spirit descend from heaven in the form of a dove and heard God's voice from heaven say, "This is my beloved Son in whom I am well pleased."

But, I believe that John the Baptist was just like you and me. When the disruption of prison occurred in his life, he found himself filled with the doubts that so easily beset each of us in times of trials. Immediately, he began to question what was going on.

God's children sometimes walk through dark, lonely places. Even when we have previously experienced God's wonderful work in our lives and others', we have lapses of faltering faith when things don't go according to our plan.

Remember the children of Israel, whom Moses led out of the bondage of Egypt? They saw the signs and plagues that God did through Moses' hand and, though reluctant at first, they were willing to follow him. They allowed him to lead them to the edge of the Red Sea. There God split the sea and allowed the Israelites to cross on dry ground to the next phase of their journey, the Promised Land. They saw the hand of God destroy the pursuing army. These same Hebrew children were provided manna in the desert, a cloud to guide them during the day and a pillar of fire for the night. They were even given quail after tiring of manna! But as we walk with them through the pages of the Word of God, we find them at the edge of the Jordan River, trembling in fear of giants.

Can you believe it? After God delivered them from Egypt, they were afraid of the giants across the river. Because of their fear and rebellion, God let them have what they wanted, even though it meant death in the wilderness, rather than an exciting walk of faith.

What did God do? He waited for the next generation.

It has always puzzled me how the people who saw God do so much could expect so little from Him again.

Then, take a look at Elijah on Mount Carmel (I Kings 18:16-45). Remember the scene on the mountain as he called fire from heaven to destroy the altar of Baal worship? What a marvelous and wonderful experience to see the hand of God act in direct response to prayer! But just a few verses later, we find Elijah running for his life from one wicked woman who just happened to be queen. No longer experiencing a "mountaintop high," he hid fearfully in a cave, doubting God could take care of his life.

Have you ever been in the same cave? Or at the same river crossing?

When things don't go like we plan, we find ourselves asking God, "Lord, are you in this? Have I done what is right? Am I being judged? What have I done wrong? Have I failed? What's it all about? Have I missed your will? Where are you, God?" Yet, as Christians we have His unfailing promise that He never slumbers nor sleeps (Psalm 121:3-4); He never leaves us (Hebrews 13:5). God can handle any of our doubts. He can deal with any of our fears and calm all of our anxieties. "For God did not give us a spirit of timidity, but a spirit of power, of love and of self-discipline" (II Timothy 1:7).

One day a man saw a team of horses pulling a very heavy load of logs. As they came to a steep place in the road, they struggled and strained, but could not move the load. The driver took several logs off and tried to start the team once again, but they still refused. He rolled off more logs, but the horses would not move. Finally, he took off every log. Then, and only then, would they begin to pull. The horses had become so discouraged by pulling with all of their strength and failing that they did not want to begin again. They had lost the desire to even try.

All of us have a hard time accomplishing anything if we have lost heart. If doubts surface in our lives, they can destroy our desire to begin again. We must cast them at the feet of Jesus as we review all His miracles in our minds, even writing them down if we must. Don't let your "giants" force you to retreat from the banks of your Jordan river and God's promised land.

The Discernment To Grasp

However, we can't stop in the tracks of discouragement; rather, we have a responsibility to respond to the encouragement of Christ.

> *Go back and report to John what you hear and see: The blind receive sight, the lame walk, those who have leprosy are cured, the deaf hear, the dead are raised, and the good news is preached to the poor."* (Matthew 11:4-5)

How exciting! Instead of focusing on the negatives, Jesus told John to look beyond the circumstances to the power of Christ and the victories already won. Notice His answer to John was different than the question that John had originally asked. John had asked, "Are you the one?", but Jesus told him to look at what God was doing now and answer his own question.

Sometimes we are filled with so many questions, doubts, and lack of confidence that we cannot see what God is doing in our lives. But our perspective of life must not be restricted to our human viewpoint. It must spring from the spiritual perspective that God gives us concerning His work in our lives. Jesus answered John's question by saying, "Look at what I am doing now." He says the same today. We have a tendency to look at Point A, our situation, and Point B, our goal. Often God is not as concerned as we are in our arriving at Point B from Point A. He is more concerned with the *process* it takes to get us from Point A to Point B. He told John to have faith in the right things, not to lose faith because of disruptions. Our eyes must be on who God is! *Our faith must be in the right things!*

Have you ever found yourself putting your hopes in your plans instead of in God's hand upon your life, trusting His sovereignty? Jesus had to teach John to discern His ways. His answer to John's question sounded more like, "Take your hands off your plans and put your hope and faith in my hand on your life." Isn't it interesting that we never fully see what God is trying to do in our lives, at least right now? Sometimes it takes years for us to discern the real plan of God. Sometimes we never know "why." But faith remains, stronger for being exercised by what we cannot see (Hebrews 11:1).

Or, perhaps you've wondered where to hand in your resignation from the rat race? The call of the wild beckons you and the adventures of a modern-day mountain man tempt you to leave for the mountains—*alone.* Or, perhaps spiritual frustration has caused you to consider an upcoming strike against God? Since you can't run away from Him, has discouragement caused you to quit serving Him? If any of this describes you, you've succumbed to the attacks of your arch-enemy—Satan. He howls with fiendish glee each time his trap of discouragement causes another believer to grow cold in his or her faith.

The story is told of a chaplain who was ministering to a dying man in World War II. He asked the young soldier if he had a message for his mother. "Yes," he said, "tell her I am dying happy." "Is there anything else?" the chaplain asked. "Would you please write my Sunday School teacher and tell her I died believing in Jesus Christ and have never forgotten all the things she taught me." Weeks later, a letter from the Sunday School teacher addressed to the chaplain arrived saying, "Oh may God have mercy upon me. Last month I quit my Sunday School class because I thought I wasn't accomplishing anything. When I got your letter telling me that my teaching had been used to win a young man to Christ, I decided to go back to my pastor and tell him that I will try again in Christ's name, being faithful to the end."

Jesus wanted John to understand that he must not focus on his broken dreams, but look at what God was doing in the midst of it and what He would do in the future. He wanted John to understand that He is the God of broken dreams as much as the God of dreams coming true. It is in the shattered rubble of broken dreams, though, that we have the greatest cause to rejoice and trust. When we observe a construction crew on our road to success, we have only one option: take His divine detour. For by those dashed hopes, we can see God giving us something better and keeping us from something less than His best.

Matthew 11:6 gives us a strange word of encouragement from the Master's lips to a man in prison: "Blessed is the man who does not fall away on account of me." John's faith was slipping because he was not flexible in God's plan for his life. Are you still in the dungeon with John? If so, don't miss the Master's answer to John, to me, and to you. He said, "Be flexible with your life." Why? Simply because God's plans for our lives may often be different from our original dreams. Sometimes, God takes us a step or two backward in order to move us a giant step forward. He wants us to understand that the experiences of "back" and "down" are not always bad in the Christian's life.

Judge Alpheus Hardy discovered his plan to be a minister was not God's plan. Later in life Hardy testified, "I wanted to go to college and become a minister, but my health broke down and the truth dawned on me that I could not be a minister. 'I cannot be God's minister' was the sentence that kept rolling in my mind. One morning, alone in my room, my distress was so great that I threw myself flat on the floor. The cry of my soul and heart was, 'O God, I cannot be your minister.' Then it came to me that I could serve God in business with the same devotion and making money for God might be my special calling. The vision was so clear and joyous, I exclaimed aloud, 'O God, I *can* be your minister. I will go back to Boston. I will make money for God and that will be my ministry. I am God's man and my ministry is to make and administer money for Him."

Choosing to use his business talents for God, he made great amounts of money and used it to support missionaries and educate ministers. The great Japanese doctor Joseph Neesima was helped by him when he landed in Boston on one of Hardy's ships. Neesima, through his work, laid the foundations of Christianity in Japan.

The best detour you may ever take could be allowing God's flexibility in your life's plans and dreams. God's detour may turn out to be better than the road you have under construction.

I'll never forget an experience I had when I pastored in Eden, Texas, my first full-time pastorate. The Sunday School attendance was sixty and in less than a year we added over a hundred new members. The news of the church's growth and the outpouring of God's Spirit in that little town spread into other towns. Eventually, a very large church in the state began to look for a pastor. I could just see me...preaching before thousands of people. But deep down in my heart, I knew it was not God's plan for my life—it was only *my* dream. Weeks later, I found that they had called one of my best friends.

I prepared and threw a grand pity party for myself. No one came except the Lord. I was preaching through the book of John during that time and in the last chapter of John, as Jesus reinstated Peter, He told him to "feed my sheep." He told Peter that a day would come when he would go where he did not want to go. Peter found himself filled with discouragement as he listened to the words of Jesus. Pointing to John, Peter said, "What about him?" Jesus looked back at Peter and said, "Peter, what's it to you if I allow him to live until I come again? You just follow me."

As I read those words, the Spirit of God penetrated to the marrow of my bones. I wept openly because God was saying to me, "What's it to you, Curt, if you pastor in this little town the rest of your life? You must follow me. What's it to you if the plans that you have made for your life do not come true? You follow me." God said "no" to me because He had a different plan for my life. Now, only a few years later, I pastor a church located in the fastest growing area of one of the fastest growing cities in the United States. The potential for outreach and ministry is beyond my previous goals. I'm glad God detoured me away from my original dream.

Many of us try to see the end before we even reach the middle. I wish I could promise you that everything will be all right as long as you follow the Lord. It may be. Yours may be a straight path leading to great success. On the other hand, it may not. It wasn't for John the Baptist...or the Apostle Paul. Both faithful servants were beheaded. Both spent the last days of their lives unjustly imprisoned.

The key to handling destroyed plans lies in one word—*blessed.* Jesus used it for John in Matthew 11:6, Job in Job 42:12, and He will use it for you and me. How? The word actually means "happiness, real joy, inward peace." God said of Job that he had spoken right of God. Have you been faithful in how you speak of the Lord?

Beverly Hills, California has more psychiatrists per square mile than any other community in the world. Yet, comedian Jackie Gleason admitted that he didn't sleep well, and Marlon Brando mused that his rise to fame and riches had increased the bank account of his psychiatrist. Elizabeth Taylor and Bridget Bardot have revealed their turmoil and frustration. Marilyn Monroe ended her life with an overdose of pills. The list goes on and on...John

Belushi, Freddie Prinze, Jimi Hendricks; the names are endless. Distraught lives filled with frustration, looking for that illusive dream of ultimate happiness. litter the pages of magazines and newspapers. *Happiness*—that's what people are really looking for! But not all the money, fame, or power in the world can provide that. It's a byproduct of *joy*—a fruit the Holy Spirit produces in the lives of Christians (Galatians 5:22-23).

If our plans for our lives do go the way we desire, but we don't honor the Lord, it won't make any difference that our plans succeeded. John the Baptist had a detour in his life I don't think he had imagined. But even as they took his life, he knew that he had lived and spent his life doing God's will. Though the detour in his life was not what he wanted or planned, he willingly accepted the will of God.

So, don't be discouraged about your present situation or condition. Real happiness and contentment in life come from trusting the Lord Jesus. His plan may not be our plan, but His are always better. We can trust Him because He loves us and desires only our best. When things don't go like the plan, creating detours and disruptions, pray for the discernment that Jesus desired John to experience: to see and accept God's plan and to follow Him even when we don't know where the detour is taking us.

Chapter 11/
Rungs on the Ladder

Be careful to follow every command I am giving you today, so that you may live and increase and may enter and possess the land that the Lord promised on oath to your forefathers. Remember how the Lord your God led you all the way in the desert these forty years, to humble you and to test you in order to know what was in your heart, whether or not you would keep his commands.

He humbled you, causing you to hunger and then feeding you with manna, which neither you nor your fathers had known, to teach you that man does not live on bread alone but on every word that comes from the mouth of the Lord. Your clothes did not wear out and your feet did not swell during these forty years. Know then in your heart that as a man disciplines his son, so the Lord your God disciplines you.

Observe the commands of the Lord your God, walking in his ways and revering him. For the Lord your God is bringing you into a good land—a land with streams and pools of water, with springs flowing in the valleys and hills; a land with wheat and barley, vines and fig trees, pomegranates, olive oil and honey; a land where bread will not be scarce and you will lack nothing; a land where the rocks are iron and you can dig copper out of the hills.

When you have eaten and are satisfied, praise the Lord your God for the good land He has given you. Be careful that you do not forget the Lord your God, failing to observe his commands, his laws and his decrees that I am giving you this day. Otherwise, when you eat and are satisfied, when you build fine houses and settle down, and when your herds and flocks grow large and your silver and gold increase and all you have is multiplied, then your heart will become proud and you will forget the Lord your God, who brought you out of Egypt, out of the land of slavery. He led you through the vast and dreadful desert, that thirsty and waterless land, with its venomous snakes and scorpions. He brought you water out of hard rock. He gave you manna to eat in the desert, something your fathers had never known, to humble and to test you so that in the end it might go well with you. You may say to yourself, "My power and the strength of my hands have produced this wealth for me." But remember the Lord your God, for it is He who gives you the ability to produce wealth, and so confirms his covenant, which He swore to your forefathers, as it is today.

If you ever forget the Lord your God and follow other gods and worship and bow down to them, I testify against you today that you will surely be destroyed. Like the nations the Lord destroyed before you, so you will be destroyed for not obeying the Lord your God.

(Deuteronomy 8)

Moses had led the people out of Egyptian bondage and through forty years of desert testing. Now, Moses tells the people "How to Stay on Top." The five basic ingredients in this passage will help us to move from the bottom up, also. This entire chapter was orginally given to the children of Israel, who, sadly, did not follow God's commands. In fact, God had to raise up a new generation under the leadership of Joshua to experience all the greatness God had for them. Even then, later generations disobeyed and found that God meant what He had said. When they practiced these five commands, they remained victorious, true winners. But the reverse was also true and is true for us as well. When we obey these commands, God guarantees that we will enjoy our "Promised Land" of godly success.

Careful Obedience

The command God gave in Deuteronomy 8:1 dictates a principle for us: *We are to be careful to follow every command of God.* When we fail, often it is because we are out of step with God; we have failed to obey. Once out of step, it doesn't take much to stumble and fall.

Moses told the people that they needed to obey the Lord carefully so they could stay in step with Him. The Lord has guidelines for every area of our lives to bless and direct us into complete success. When we fail to follow the Father's commands, condemnation occurs, then judgment follows.

Could God say the following words to you? To me? To any of His people today? They should cause spiritual sobriety.

Ye call me Master and obey me not;
Ye call me Light and see me not;
Ye call me Way and walk not;
Ye call me Life and desire me not;
Ye call me Wise and follow me not;
Ye call me Fair and love me not;
Ye call me Rich and ask me not;
Ye call me Eternal and seek me not;
Ye call me Gracious and trust me not;
Ye call me Noble and serve me not;
Ye call me Mighty and honor me not;

> *Ye call me Just and fear me not;*
> *If I condemn you, BLAME ME not!*
> —Unknown[1]

The Lord wants us to obey Him as *His* child first, so that all goes well in our earthly family and in our earthly relationships. He wants us to follow Him—and His ethics—in our business life, so that our business is blessed as well. He desires our trust in His riches rather than in our finances so that our financial weather vane doesn't swing in the winds of the world's materialism. And He desires us to trust Him with our emotions, so they do not toss us to and fro. Every area of our life demands obedience or we, too, will be destroyed by the enemy.

If we are not careful, we can easily give Satan a foothold in our lives. It's then that we find ourselves defeated. For instance, suppose you own a Texas-size ranch of acres and acres. But right in the center of your ranch is a little one acre plot that the owner consistently refuses to sell to you. In some states, the law allows access to that one, lone spot. In fact, the owner of that spot has a legal right to build a road through your surrounding land to get to his property. The same is true for us as Christians. If we leave any area uncontrolled by the Father, the devil will take steps to reach that self-contained area in our lives. That's why we need to obey carefully, so that we do not stumble and give Satan an easy access into our lives.

Continuous Awareness

When we encounter problems, we need to be aware of how they can be used and are being used by God in our lives. We need to look positively at what they do for us.

First, *problems reveal our heart.* Deuteronomy 8:2

declares that the desert experience revealed the hearts of the people. When we walk through problems, our hearts, our feelings, "the real us" float to the top. That's how it was with the Israelite people. After forty years in the desert, they saw a picture of their hearts, and it wasn't pretty.

The next time you experience a problem, observe your attitude. It's a mirror of your heart. Like the desert experience of the Israelites, your problems may be God's testing grounds for you. Usually, it's not until a tough situation occurs in our lives that we understand that we have a heart problem that needs to be confessed, changed, and forgiven.

Second, *problems redirect our mind.* God also uses problems in our lives to redirect our minds and attention. Verse 3 of Deuteronomy 8 teaches us that God wants us to understand, "Man does not live on bread alone but on every word that comes from the mouth of the Lord."

What does that mean? It is in the midst of those critical situations that we need to remember that problems come in order to redirect our minds to God's Word. When all else fails, read the instructions!

Problems also redirect our minds to affirm proper values. They reveal to us what we consider important in our lives. God used the problem of food in the lives of the Israelites to refocus their minds on Him and their dependence upon Him.

In the same way, problems also can reveal emptiness in our lives—and show us that a personal relationship with Christ is the most valuable gift in the world. Problems help us reach that realization again and again.

Third, *problems refine our faith.* Through forty years of desert hiking, the Israelites' clothes did not wear out and their feet did not swell. God taught them through time and experience that He is the One who could meet all of their needs, focusing their faith for daily provision upon Him.

When we face problems, we often find that we can't take care of even our most basic needs. We learn again through a fresh experience that God, and God alone, supplies all our needs.

When my wife and I married, we had no washing machine or dryer. She had to drive several miles to a laundromat, so we began to pray about our "dirty clothes problem." We had already picked out a particular washing machine and dryer, praying that God would supply the funds to make the purchase. When I read Philippians 4:19, I claimed it for us. "And my God will meet all your needs according to his glorious riches in Christ Jesus."

A month later on a Saturday morning, there was a knock at our door. My wife answered the door, and it was a delivery man from Sears. They had a delivery to make: one washing machine and one dryer. Not just any washer and dryer, but the very same ones that we had selected. No one knew that we had looked at Sears. No one knew that we had a specific color that we wanted. No one knew that we were waiting for God to supply the money. But God knew and apparently told one of His saints about our need. To this day, we still do not know who His supplier was. But that experience refined our faith because we learned that God cares about seemingly insignificant things and uses those to instruct His children. Not even our financial crisis was too difficult. Believe me, you can trust God for everything.

God may not choose to answer as He did in this instance, but you can be sure He's on top of your problem. "In this you greatly rejoice, though now for a little while you may have had to suffer grief in all kinds of trials.

These have come so that your faith—of greater worth than gold, which perishes even though refined by fire—may be proved genuine and may result in praise, glory and honor when Jesus Christ is revealed" (I Peter 1:6-7).

Fourth, *problems often reassure our sonship.* "Know then in your heart that as a man disciplines his son, so the Lord your God disciplines you" (Deuteronomy 8:5). "My son, do not make light of the Lord's discipline, and do not lose heart when he rebukes you, because the Lord disciplines those he loves, and he punishes everyone he accepts as a son" (Hebrews 12:5-6).

Discipline is a critical responsibility of parenthood, a necessary responsibility. We discipline children so they will learn to obey and to give them safe, secure boundaries wherein they can exercise their personal freedom. That's exactly what happened during the desert experience. The people had disobeyed God by not believing Him and going into the Promised Land when they should have. Now, after forty years and with a new generation, God gave them a new opportunity. He never gave up on them for they were still His children. The Lord's discipline reassured their sonship. The limitations they saw on His permissiveness assured them that He was in control.

This awareness that problems reassure our sonship is felt in our hearts. The biblical writer of Deuteronomy even begins the sentence with the words, "Know then in your heart..." (8:5). Words cannot adequately express the deep, heartfelt emotions of parental love and concern, especially in the area of discipline. The often quoted phrase, "This is going to hurt me more than it's going to hurt you," really is true. And, strangely, I have found, as a parent, that after a discipline session with one of my children has occurred, their desire to be with me and to experience my affection is even greater than before the session occurred. I have no desire for the responsibility to discipline my neighbor's children. I do want my children to act in a godly manner and to obey the rules of the house, laws of society, and, more importantly, God's requirements for their lives. Our heavenly Father wants the same of us.

In that climb to the top from the pits of despair, or on the ladder of success, the believer must always be aware of what problems accomplish. And the battle between the ears must never be underestimated—for that's where the war of continuous awareness is fought.

Conscientious Praise

In verse 10, Moses tells the people that when they have eaten and are satisfied, "Praise the Lord your God for the good land he has given you." We must never ignore praise because it keeps our minds focused on the Father. When you praise the Lord, you give him credit for what He has done in your life. Praise is personal adoration of God, acknowledging who He is and what He is doing. As we praise God, we allow our lips and minds to express what our hearts know to be true.

When I was growing up, there were two phrases which my parents made sure I knew and used. One was "please," and the other was "thank you." We certainly know how to say "please" to God. Most of our prayers are filled with,"Please, God, give me this," and "Please, God, give me that." But too often we forget to say, "Thank you." Conscientious, continuous praise keeps our minds saying "thank you" to the Lord.

I once heard a story about a young man in Germany who was on a hospital operating table. The surgeon, being observed by a group of his students, leaned over the patient and said, "Do you wish to say anything? You have the opportunity, but as you know, these words will be the last that you'll ever utter." The young man had cancer of the tongue and the operation was to remove that organ from his body. "Please think well about what you wish to say," encouraged the surgeon. A long silence occurred as the young man was lost in deep thought. A reverent awareness settled over the crowd. What words would he choose for his last utterance? Eagerly they waited. Eventually, he opened his mouth and at the sound of his voice, tears began to flow throughout the operating room as he declared, "Thank God. . .Jesus Christ." Just the beautiful name "Jesus" is praise. Keep His name in your mind. Keep His name on your lips. It will help you to remember who you are and whose you are.

Constant Remembrance

The last half of Deuteronomy 8 is specifically written to ensure that God's people stay in a state of constant remembrance. Verse 11 warns, "Be careful that you do not forget the Lord your God."

Whether making the journey from the bottom up or just trying to stay afloat, there are several things that must never be forgotten.

Remember Who Is Blessing You

Pride may convince us that we have produced successful results ourselves. Self-deceived, we believe that the climb to fame, fortune, and personal accomplishment has only been made possible by our self-fortitude and determination. But Deuteronomy 8:18 reminds us that it is God who gives us the ability to produce wealth or success. He gives it freely and can take it away just as quickly. It is often because we fail to remember who truly provides our resources that we lose them. God tells us, "Command those who are rich in this present world not to be arrogant nor to put their hope in wealth, which is so uncertain, but to put their hope in God, who richly provides us with everything for our enjoyment. Command them to do good, to be rich in good deeds, and to be generous and willing to share" (I Timothy 6:17-18).

It has been said that "a self-made man often worships his own creator." By constantly remembering who is blessing us, we can avoid self-idolization and the ultimate failure that it brings just as I Timothy 6:9-10 warns: "People who want to get rich fall into temptation and a trap and into many foolish and harmful desires that plunge men into ruin and destruction. For the love of money is a root of all kinds of evil. Some people, eager for money, have wandered from the faith and pierced themselves with many griefs" (I Timothy 6:9-10).

Remember Who You Are and Where You've Come From

Sometimes, when God blesses us with material things or prosperity, we think and act like God had nothing to do with it; we forget who we are and from where we've come. Have you ever observed the actions of those who have nothing, and then suddenly acquire great wealth? Sometimes they get social amnesia, forgetting old friends. Or, it may well be that they desire to forget their humble beginnings. To be authentic as a Christian, though, don't shun the people of your past when you jettison the debris of yesteryear.

By constant remembrance of who we are and where we have come from, humility becomes a positive attribute in our lives.

Remember The Lord

Throughout Deuteronomy 8, Moses reiterates, "Remember the Lord." Some might wonder how anyone can forget the Lord. But it's easy. When you think more about yourself and what you have than who has given it, a lack of spiritual awareness follows. When your position and possessions become more important to you than Whose you are, it's easy to forget the Lord. That's why Moses warned, "Don't forget Him. Remember, don't forget the Lord."

In verse 17, Moses gives a warning signal to describe someone who has forgotten the Lord. You may say to yourself, " 'my power and the strength of my hands have produced this wealth for me'." Notice the number of personal pronouns in the one sentence: "my power...my hands...for me." Sounds a lot like the rich fool the Lord describes for us in Luke 12:16-21.

Let's face it. When we arrive on top of life's heap, we are tempted to give a personal testimony of, "How I succeeded by myself." It's a natural, sinful weakness to think and to believe that we have done it all. Usually, it's only when we sink to the bottom that we cry out for God's help, conscious that we cannot succeed without Him.

If we follow the biblical history of the rise and fall and rise of the Israelite people, we see that their prosperity parallels total commitment to the Lord. When they were committed, honoring Him, they were successful. But, when they failed to follow God, remembered only the works of their own hands, and focused on *their* prosperity, they fell to the bottom—just like God promised them would happen: "If you ever forget the Lord your God and follow other gods and worship and bow down to them, I testify against you today that you will surely be destroyed. Like the nations the Lord destroyed before you, so you will be destroyed for not obeying the Lord your God" (Deuteronomy 8:19-20). If we want to succeed, to be winners, we must constantly remember the Lord and obey Him.

Remember The Consequences Of Sin
  Sin has personal consequences. It's a fact we often choose to ignore. James Nankivell has listed twenty-five things we can't do without consequences:
1. Sow bad habits and reap a good character.
2. Sow jealousy and hatred and reap love and friendship.
3. Sow wicked thoughts and reap a clean life.
4. Sow wrong deeds and live righteously.
5. Sow crime and get away with it.
6. Sow dissipation and reap a healthy body.
7. Sow crooked dealings and succeed indefinitely.
8. Sow self-indulgence and not show it in your face.
9. Sow disloyalty and reap loyalty from others.
10. Sow dishonesty and reap integrity.
11. Sow profane words and reap clean speech.
12. Sow disrespect and reap respect.
13. Sow deception and reap confidence.
14. Sow untidiness and reap neatness.
15. Sow intemperance and reap sobriety and temperance.
16. Sow indifference and reap nature's rewards.
17. Sow mental or physical laziness and reap a responsible position in society.
18. Sow cruelty and reap kindness.
19. Sow wastefulness and reap thriftiness.
20. Sow cowardice and reap courage.
21. Sow destruction of other people's property and reap protection for our own.
22. Sow greed and envy and reap generosity.

23. Sow neglect of the Lord's house and reap strength in temptation.
24. Sow neglect of the Bible and reap a well-guided life.
25. Sow human thistles and reap human roses.²

I would add one more to the list above: We cannot sow self-confidence, self-assurance, and self-centeredness and reap salvation. The consequences of sin are devastating.

A young man, still living at home, lived a life of dissipation and drunkenness. Over the years, his saintly mother fought thousands of prayerful battles for him. One night, coming up the stairs in a drunken stupor, he glanced into his mother's room. He saw her on her knees, weeping as she called his name aloud in prayer. Her prayer was a simple one, "God, give him a desire to repent of sin and turn in faith to Jesus." It was the first time he had ever heard his mother pray for him. In brokenness and tears, he fell by his mother's side and gave his life to Christ. It was a joyous reunion as mother and son experienced spiritual unity because of Jesus' death on the cross. Her years of prayers were finally answered as the son made his first step to life in Christ.

As he turned to walk out of her room, he noticed on the back of her door a carving of a heart with nails driven inside the lines. Hundreds of nails covered the heart. "Mother, what is that?" he asked.

She said, "Son, that has been my heart these many years. Each nail has been a day that you have broken my heart, living as you have. But now I am so happy that you have given your life to Christ."

With tears in his eyes, he said, "Take the nails out of your heart, Mom. I'll never live like that again!"

"Everyday that you live a life that's Christ-like, I'll take a nail out," the old saint replied.

"Oh, Mom, I can't wait for the day when there are no more of my nails in your heart," he said.

Weeks and months passed and one by one the nails were removed. Finally, the long awaited day came. Taking her son by the arm, the mother directed him to the back of her door and said, "Look, the nails are all gone. They are gone, son. I am so proud of you." She looked into his face expecting a radiant smile, but saw tears flowing like mountain streams down his face. "What's wrong?" she asked. "I thought you would be happy! The nails are all gone."

In tearful, broken words, he replied, "I know, Mom, but the holes are still there."

God can and does remove the guilt and penalty of sin from our lives, but the consequences must still be borne by the trespasser. Only in heaven will we be fully free of sin's consequences, guaranteed of it through Jesus Christ.

Why does God encourage us to remain pure? It is not only for the purpose of maintaining fellowship with Him, but also so that we will be spared sin's consequences.

If you desire to climb the ladder of godly success, never forget: There is no sin without a consequence.

Courageous Vision

Located between a verse of righteous encouragement and one of promise is a verse of vision. Deuteronomy 8:7 declares, "For the Lord your God is bringing you into a good land." Nothing will allow you to climb the ladder of godly success faster, win sooner, or stay on top longer than having a courageous vision. A courageous vision is one that believes, "God is going to bless me—*His way.*"

Far too many people look behind every problem, believing that God wants them to be miserable, when His real desire is to bless us, fellowship with us, and to make us winners. . .by being the central focus of our lives.

Just like the Israelites, God wants to lead us from the desert experiences of life to godly success. The Wilderness of Zin was never God's perfect plan for the children of Israel. It was only a place to pass through in order to reach the Promised Land. We must not let ourselves get trapped in the Wilderness of Sin because of cowardly advisors or personal failures. Our spiritual eyesight must focus on the physical reality of God's desires for us. When that happens, a courageous vision blossoms inside each winner's soul, producing a confidence that God will bring us into a bountiful land of His choosing.

Perhaps there are dark clouds and dreary moments that hover over you right now. Be confident that at the right time and place, God *will* catch your eye—if you're looking at Him—and show you the next step. He wants you to have a courageous vision, one that sees Him blessing you. Follow that vision! Don't move out into the fast lane of life without looking His way.

Notes:
[1] Taken from *Encyclopedia of 7700 Illustrations* by Paul Lee Tan, ThD., Assurance Publishers. Used with permission
[2] *Ibid.*

Chapter 12/ Doing The Impossible

> ". . .For nothing is impossible with God" (Luke 1:37).

A few years ago there was a television show called, "That's Incredible." Week after week average people accomplished the seemingly impossible. I'll never forget the first time I saw the program. On the screen was a club from England who got together to do strange things. This program showed them on Colorado's Royal Gorge Bridge in "tails" and top hats. They had tied huge bungi cords to their legs, and one after the other jumped off the bridge that spans the Arkansas River more than 1,000 feet below. Reaching the end of the elastic rope, each one bounced wildly while hanging upside down until a helicopter came to the rescue. Across the television screen flashed the words, "That's Incredible!" Though incredibly stupid to me, it was still incredible. All kinds of things were done by people doing impossible things.

If humans in their limited physical capabilities can do the incredible, how much more should the people of God seek to do impossible things for the kingdom of God? We, who are believers, are supercharged with the very Spirit of God. His desire is for us to accomplish the impossible for Him.

It is a sad commentary on twentieth century Christianity when we see churches with no power. Unfortunately, some congregations are about as exciting as perfume without scent because their programs are dull and traditional. What they do is usually only a copy of what someone else has done before them. A church or even a business may have potential, but unless there is a vision, burning deep within, it will fail to become successful. For many, the essential, missing ingredient is an all-consuming desire to see God's "impossible" happen in their lives.

Nothing electrifies a Christian more than having the impossible happen in a personal way. Mary, soon to be the mother of Jesus, had it happen to her. She was never again the same. The early church experienced the impossible, and it rocked the world with the truth of God. Paul experienced it and wrote almost half the New Testament. Martin Luther experienced it and changed the course of church history. Nothing will turn a church or personal life around as much as cultivating that desire to have the impossible happen...and allowing ourselves to be God's channel to accomplish it. Believe it will happen, and you'll be that winner God always intended for you to become.

So what can we do to make the impossible happen in our lives, businesses, families, or churches? If we take the following principles and put them into practice, we will see that truly nothing is impossible with God.

Develop the Impossible

How is that possible? How can we put every issue, every problem, every situation, and every circumstance in our lives into a framework of the impossible? Begin to develop a mentality of the impossible; desire it to become reality, centered within the boundaries of God's ability. Every situation that enters our boundaries of life and every goal that we seek to accomplish, regardless of how big or how small, should be considered in terms of the impossible and the God of the impossible. When we develop that concept in our lives, we reaffirm our confidence that the God who created the stars and galaxies is the same one working on our behalf.

Many people never experience the impossible becoming a reality in their lives because they fail to think about it consistently and, therefore, they never develop that confidence in who God really is. Call it *im*possibility thinking: A mindset of looking for what *God* wants you to accomplish and saying, "I want to experience that in my life!"

Maybe you have a fantastic dream that God has given you. But right now, it appears totally impossible. Get excited about its very impossibility! If God wishes it to become a reality in your life, when it does, your faith in Him and your testimony of His power will soar as never before. As you develop this vision of doing the impossible, begin to look at all its ingredients. Ask, "Father, what do you want me to do? Give me the vision that *you* desire me to see. Give me your dream of what *you* want me to accomplish. Give me the desires of *your* heart as my heart's desire." Don't just exist week after week doing the same old thing, keeping the *status quo,* quoed! One day you'll wake up with the realization that the rut you dug has become your grave.

If we want something exciting to happen, we must learn to develop *im*possibility thinking through a godly mentality. God says He is able "to do immeasurably more than all we ask or imagine, according to his power" (Ephesians 3:20). Remember Mary's question to Gabriel, the messenger of God, when he told her that she would bear the Son of God (Luke 1:31-34)? Immediately, she asked, "How will this be since I am a virgin?" The angel answered, "Nothing is impossible with God." Clearly, he was saying to her and to each Christian in the centuries since, "God can do anything." But notice, too, Mary's acceptance of this "impossibility." "I am the Lord's servant. May it be to me as you have said." She didn't question, doubt, or consider the difficulties this announcement would bring into her life. She humbly accepted—and believed that God knew what He was doing and was in control.

Look at your life. Look at your church. Look at your job, friends, relationships, dreams. Are you happy with what you are, what you're doing, and what is being accomplished in your life? Or, is the "go for it" mentality absent? Are you missing out on your dream of success?

We have a young couple in our church who won a home on the television program "Dream House." They moved to our town because the house was given to them. And that's why we enter all of the crazy drawings and sweepstakes, realizing the slim chances of winning, still we think, "It might be me next time. It might be me! I want to win that truck, car, or house. I want that ten million dollar jackpot. It could be me."

Our society is filled with that sense of expectation. It is part of our emotional make-up. Who put it there? God. But instead of letting that desire be twisted by the world, we need to allow the Lord to mold it. Begin with the desire to experience a closer walk with the Lord. Add to that a life-changing dare to live all-out for Jesus Christ. Then begin to develop the avenues for God to make you a winner: Prayer, Bible study, church attendance, fellowship with other believers, witnessing. You won't find that God gives us something for nothing. Commitment, faith, trust—all require effort. But they are the substance of seeing the impossible become reality in your life.

Even the growth of Metropolitan Baptist Church in Houston, Texas is the result of developing the impossible. While the church was running about three hundred in Sunday School, the church's Long-Range Planning Committee decided to build the largest worship center they could on their 11.5 acres. One was designed that could eventually hold four thousand people at a cost of five million dollars. They heard the Lord's instruction, "Go for it," clearly. Not knowing how they were going to pay for it, they trusted Him. Though there were no millionaires in the church, the heart of the body cried out, "Let's do it!" I'm humbled by the opportunity to pastor such a people who have learned to believe in the impossible—and the God of the impossible. I believe with all my heart that that is what the Father wants for each of us. Allow Him to energize your dreams, making the impossible become reality.

There are many churches who are so organized, programmed, and computerized, they have already figured out what they can do and when they can do it. They select pastors by running their personality traits and the congregation's desires through a computer—instead of the Holy Spirit. Many Christians are just like that with their lives. They have already programmed out the impossible. What they *do* believe God can do, they have already figured how it can be done or how *they* can do it. *Their* accomplishments become the probable, and God's work in the fulfillment becomes minimal.

If that's not for you, then take a second step:

Dream the Impossible

Most of us have lost the ability to dream godly dreams.

If *you* have, re-learn the ability by reading the Bible. The New Testament tells a wonderful story of a beggar who knew how to dream (Mark 10:46-52). Blind Bartimaeus sat on the side of the road, probably with a group of other beggars. When he heard that Jesus of Nazareth was passing by him, he shouted to Him...but not for money. Bartimaeus had an urgent request for something far more precious than money.

As Jesus, His disciples, and a large crowd filled the road, blind Bartimaeus began to cry out, "Jesus, Son of David, have mercy on me!" Many told the beggar, "Shut up, Bartimaeus." But the Bible says that he wouldn't listen to them. Instead, he began to shout even louder, "Jesus, Son of David, have mercy on me!" Finally, Jesus stopped, turned around, and looked at the insistent beggar. Then, the Son of God asked him a leading question, "What do you want me to do for you?"

Bartimaeus dared to ask what no one else had ever requested from Christ: "I want to see," he said. It had never been done before. In fact, it was taught that only God could restore sight. There were no optometrists or ophthalmologists. Eye surgery was unknown. But Bartimaeus had an appointment with The Great Physician! Here was a man with enough faith to dream—and believe—the impossible. "I want to see!" And he did.

What do you want in your life that's impossible? Do you desire to accomplish anything that's unlikely? Do you even have a dream? If you don't, then it will never occur. That's the first step to seeing the impossible happen. Dare to dream.

Jesus gave His disciples an impossible dream.

I have called you friends, for everything that I have learned from my Father I have made known to you. You did not choose me, but I chose you to go and bear fruit—fruit that will last.... When the Counselor comes, whom I will send to you from the Father...."

(John 15:15-16, 26)

"You will receive power when the Holy Spirit comes on you; and you will be my witnesses in Jerusalem, and in all Judea and Samaria, and to the ends of the earth."

(Acts 1:8)

I'm sure those promises and that commission seemed an impossibility to them. But it wasn't. We are still sharing in them today. The seemingly impossible may just be God's plan for our lives. He wants us to believe, work, and wait for Him to make our dreams come true.

If you don't have a dream right now, or are afraid to have one, ask God to give you one. A dream is one of the most important things in life. Sometimes God uses things that come into our lives such as critical needs and difficult circumstances, just like Bartimaeus had, to produce a dream. Had he not been blind, he would not have had a desire to see.

But, you can't stop there, you must take another step.

Listen to the Impossible

Raised by Eli the priest, young Samuel learned to listen to God. While sleeping in the temple one night, God called him by name (I Samuel 3). "Samuel. Samuel." The boy thought it was Eli and went to him. "Here I am." But Eli said, "I didn't call you; go back to sleep." After this occurred a third time, Eli realized that God was trying to speak to little Samuel.

Eli told Samuel, "If the voice of the Lord speaks to you again, reply by saying, 'Speak, Lord, for your servant is listening.' " The voice of the Lord did come again. This time Samuel did exactly what Eli said, responding, "Speak, for your servant is listening." When he realized it was the Lord calling him, he was ready to listen and obey.

It's sad that so many people miss seeing the impossible happen in their lives because they have failed to listen. Psalm 46:10 says, "Be still and know that I am God." We must listen to God if we want to know Him. If we don't listen, we might "do our own thing" and miss the "best thing." Remember, God's impossibilities are greater than our dreams, but we must listen to Him. That's why a quiet time of prayer and Bible study is critical to a healthy Christian life.

Have you ever had something happen to the hand you normally use? I did. My right ring finger had a head-on collision with a softball. I found myself in a real dilemma. I was going to have to use my left hand in ways I never had before. But even though my left hand was willing and open to suggestions, I found that it was a bit uncoordinated. The next couple of weeks were somewhat trying—especially when trying to shave my face!

But isn't that similar to the Christian life? We depend upon things and people. . .and then all of a sudden that "crutch" is put out of commission. It is true that you never fully appreciate something until you lose it—whether it's the use of a muscle, an arm, or a hand. Spiritually, we often use man-made crutches, too, instead of following the God-given regimen of exercise that keeps us spiritually fit. I recommend strenuous, daily exercise of the following in order to make your spiritual muscles those of a true winner.

Prayer. Have no doubts about it; it is the strongest limb upon which we can depend. This is where our wars are fought and our victories won. To be strong, it must be exercised frequently, powerfully. Prayer must be a familiar strength in your life *before you need it.* For the day will come (if it hasn't already) when you will need to depend upon prayer and prayer alone. Prayer is the muscle of faith. It is where we stretch, dream, petition, and intercede before the throne of God. The more we pray, the better we get at it. The better we get at it, the more relaxed we will feel when we approach our heavenly Father with the needs—and praises!—of our life. Too often, we let prayer become the brass ring on life's carousel, only reaching for it when there is a crisis in our lives. Then, we find that when we must depend on it, we are too weak to grab hold of its strength. Prayer muscles must be exercised daily.

Have you ever found yourself immobilized spiritually? Prayer can take care of the greatest needs in your life, but it's a major muscle in the Christian life that grows weak from lack of use when we let everything else come between us and intimate conversation with the Lord. Exercise it today and listen to God. First Thessalonians 5:17 commands us, "Pray continually." There's a reason for that.

It's easy to talk to people about walking with God—and fail to do it ourselves. Even ministers get so busy doing the work of ministry that we can fail to have a quiet time on a consistent basis. Do you know God's voice? Have you ever wondered how to know when God is guiding you? If He spoke to you today, would you know it was the Lord?

I can hear my wife's voice in a crowd. Why? Because I spend time with her, listening to her. I'm familiar with her laugh and the tone of her voice. Spend time with the Lord—and you'll be able to hear Him clearly when He talks to you.

Create the Impossible

Don't be afraid when God creates or allows impossible situations in your life. Often, we struggle to be so organized that there is hardly room for life's creative circumstances to be realized. We have already predetermined our goals, and we have asked God to bless our boredom. Even if we call our objective impossible, we have already planned for it to be probable. But if we accomplish the probable, *we* receive the glory. But, when God accomplishes impossible things in our lives, *He* receives the glory. Many times He creates the impossible by putting us face-to-face with an unsolvable situation just so we can exercise our faith, strengthen our trust, and see Him work in our lives. He gives us opportunities to praise and honor Him.

In Judges 7, the Midianites are once again harassing the Israelites. One Israelite man, Gideon, was tired of always being on the run, and God put into his heart a desire to force the Midianites out of Israel. Every year, the marauding tribe took what they wanted. Gideon, almost like a cheerleader, assembled Israel and urged them to attack the Midianites. Thirty-two thousand Israelites rallied to Gideon's side. They were ready for battle. Victory was assured—until God said he had too many soldiers. Gideon was shocked, but he was listening. Under the direction of the Lord, Gideon told the men who were afraid to go home. Twenty-two thousand said, "We'll pray for you in our own homes." That left only ten thousand to fight the battle. But God spoke to Gideon again saying, "You still have too many." Gideon said, "Lord, there are only ten thousand of us against hundreds of thousands of them."

"Trust me," came the reply.

God's Selective Service program continued after a twenty mile hike. Everyone was thirsty and as they came to a river, those who dropped down on their knees to drink were sent home. Now, of the thirty-two thousand who had originally said, "Let's destroy the Midianites," God had chosen only three hundred for Gideon to lead. Three hundred against thousands. Now, *that's* impossible! Why did God do that? Why did God create the impossible for Gideon's three hundred? Simply...so that He would get the glory.

Don't be afraid of impossible situations. If you can succeed based upon what you and all the technology, planning, organization, and help from friends can do, it brings no honor to the Lord. But if the situation is beyond human help, it focuses our attention upon the awesome power of God.

God created an impossible circumstance with potentially fatal consequences in Gideon's life. And God creates a platform on which the faith of each of His children can stand—for the world to see. With our backs against the wall of life, we are positioned for Him to reveal His hand. Maybe you're walking through a tough situation right now. Possibly, you find it hard to think about deliverance or success because the odds are so great against you. If so, you have the very ingredient the Father wants: an impossible situation. Don't shake with fear! Get excited! You're on the most adventurous road that you could ever travel...the impossible. The road signs and service stations are few, but faith will make sure you get there.

But let's change the metaphor and look at another essential element. Once the Father gives direction to the ship of your life, you must set sail. Two men in the Old Testament come to mind in this regard: Noah and Abraham. As you look at their lives, you'll notice a word synonymous with their names, *obedience.*

Noah was willing to obey the impossible—even the unheard of. One day, the Master Builder of the universe told him exactly how to build an ark (Genesis 5-6)—and added a new word to his vocabulary. After a detailed explanation of the boat he would build, Noah started to work on it. People laughed at him, too; for one hundred and twenty years they mocked him as he preached and built the first zoo. But, the impossible things that God told Noah to do saved his life, his family's lives, and the future of the world. Why? Because he was willing to obey the impossible, doing what had never been done before.

One of the most suspenseful stories in the Old Testament is God's command to Abraham to sacrifice his son, Isaac (Genesis 22). A miracle child, and a child of promise, Isaac was Sarah and Abraham's pride and joy. But then came God's command: Abraham was to offer Isaac as a burnt offering.

Imagine the doubts, the questions, the possible rebellion that could have flared up in Abraham's heart and mind. But he went, confident that God had a plan. And when Isaac asked his father where the sacrifice was, the answer came clearly and confidently, "God Himself will provide a sacrifice."

But even as they climbed the mount, built the altar, collected the firewood, no escape from his seemingly impossible situation occurred. In obedience, Abraham bound Isaac, placed him on the altar, and raised the knife to slay him. As the tension built to a nerve shattering point, an angel of the Lord called out and told him to stop! It had only been a test...and Abraham passed with flying colors!

"I swear by myself, declares the Lord, that because you have done this and have not withheld your son, your only son, I will surely bless you and make your descendants as numerous as the stars in the sky and as the sand on the seashore. Your descendants will take possession of the cities of their enemies, and through your offspring all nations on earth will be blessed, *because you have obeyed me*" (Genesis 22:16-18, emphasis mine).

Now *that's* ultimate success!

Abraham did not understand God's commands, but he didn't question, he didn't allow rebellion or anger to build up inside of him. He obeyed. He said, "Okay, Lord, I don't understand, but I'll do it your way."

We, too, must have this mindset, to obey God and live our lives His way, by His commands. It made Abraham a winner; our faith and trust will do the same for us.

Share the Impossible

Often, God wants us to share in the impossible by agreeing with one another in prayer. It has been said that unless we share a dream with others, it stagnates.

As pastor, I was concerned about raising enough money to build the worship center at our church. I shared my doubts, concerns, and dreams with one of my faithful deacons—who put his arm around me and said, "Pastor, that's not just your dream. It's our dream, too!" The name of our building program was "Share the Vision," and I discovered that it was true!

A prayer partner is a welcomed companion as you walk the street called impossible. God may give you a fabulous dream, but you must never hold onto it selfishly. Mary, the mother of Jesus, shared with her cousin, Elizabeth, the impossible dream that God was making a reality through her. She shared it with Joseph, and it became their dream together. Find a significant friend or a group of people who care about you and share your impossibility with them. When God works, others will be able to rejoice more intimately in the beauty of your life and God's power.

Pray the Impossible

As you're sharing, don't forget to pray for the impossible. I love the story of Elijah and the prophets of Baal in the "Showdown at Mt. Carmel" (I Kings 18). Elijah prayed the impossible. He didn't want an easy, ordinary victory. No way! After preparing the altar, he had it drenched with water, *then* he asked God to come and destroy the sacrifice. He declared "You, O Lord, are God!" God answered with fire, accepting the sacrifice and the honor due Him. Search Scripture and you'll never find God telling Elijah to do it that way. But, that didn't stop Elijah! He believed God could do anything.

Our heavenly Father has a flare for the dramatic. He created man from a handful of dust. He parted the Red Sea and dropped manna from heaven. His Son walked on water and fed five thousand people with just a sack lunch. God's Word reveals to us that He loves to do impossible things. Just think of your own salvation and the awesome impossibility of saving a human soul from eternal hell. Hebrews 13:8 says, "Jesus Christ is the same yesterday and today and forever." We can be confident that His desires are the same now as they were in the Old Testament and last week. He is waiting for His children to pray the impossible. Don't try to program the impossible—just pray it and believe it. God has equipped us "with everything good for doing his will" (Hebrews 13:21).

Pay the Impossible

Daniel paid an expensive price for honoring his commitment to serve God and breaking the laws of the land of Babylon (Daniel 6). He refused to pray to the king and because of his rebellion, he was brought before Darius. The king had no recourse but to send him to his death. It's hard to know what Daniel's thoughts were as he fell helplessly into that Babylonian lions' den. His faithfulness to God had met its ultimate test.

Sometimes, we must put our lives on the line for God. But if God's "possible" is our heart's "impossible" desire, it *will* cost us something.

During my seminary years, I had a professor who continually pointed his finger at our class while he taught. I'm sure you know the kind. One day he said, "You know, men, I've got one fear and one fear only." The class sat up and listened intently. "One of these days when I die and go to heaven, my greatest fear is that Jesus will look at me, shake His head, and say, 'I had so much more for you. Why didn't you ask?' " Those words have haunted me over the years. I have finally come to the place where I want the Lord to say to me on that day, "Curt, I really didn't have planned for you all that you expected me to do. But because you were willing to trust me and pay the price, I gave you more."

How about you? Wouldn't you rather expect too much of Jesus, than too little of Him? It's more biblical to presume on God's ability than never to risk anything. If there was ever a word we need to hear today, it is that we must be willing to pay the cost to see God's impossibles happen in our lives, our hearts, our minds. Is there an addiction you need to break? A habit you need to conquer? A change you need to make? It will cost you something as you stretch for those God-given dreams, but when you see God do the impossible in your life, you'll know it was worth the price.

Believe the Impossible

In Matthew 8:5-13, a Roman centurion asked Jesus to heal his servant. Jesus said, "I will go and heal him." But the man told Jesus, "Lord, I do not deserve to have you come under my roof. But just say the word, and my servant will be healed." He didn't need to see Jesus lay His hands on the servant. He didn't need the prestige of having the Rabbi in his home. He knew that Jesus was so powerful that all He had to do was speak the words and the servant would be healed.

Are you one of those people who wants to see something before believing it? Are you residing in the spiritual state of Missouri where you challenge God by saying, "Show me!"? The centurion believed the impossible. You can, too. "Faith is being sure of what we hope for and certain of what we do not see" (Hebrews 11:1). It has been said that "faith is that ability to walk to the edge of all the light you have and be willing to take one step more, believing that God will either give you firm ground on which to step—or wings to fly."

Our faith is based upon the Word of God, the Bible. There are hundreds of promises for the believer throughout the pages of God's Book. More than enough for us to trust Him. God keeps His word, and the record of His faithfulness is ours to see.

As I've already shared, in the early days of our marriage, we claimed Philippians 4:19, "And my God will meet all your needs according to His glorious riches in Christ Jesus," when we were in need of a washer and dryer. But still another problem raised its head: transportation.

I was driving to Fort Worth to go to the seminary, and my wife was working in Dallas while also attending school. We were in a fix with only one car. I knew how God had taken care of the washing machine and dryer, so I innocently figured that He could handle our automobile problem as well. I went to car lots daily looking for the right car for our family. I had no money and little credit, but I knew that God would provide one way or another, even if He had to personally coerce a banker into giving me a loan. I figured that God would provide an extra job or something else to meet the need. It was the "something else" that God did. Once again, something I hadn't expected, but which fit perfectly in the context of God's Philippians 4:19 promise.

One day, John Trantham, a good friend, came to my door. When I answered the door, John was standing there with a set of car keys held out toward me. I said, "What's this for?" He said, "You'll never believe this, Curt, but today I was driving to work, asking God what I should do about my third car. It's a 1967 Chrysler 300, you know, and as I prayed about what to do with it, whether to sell it or keep it, God clearly told me to give it to you. Here are the keys." I could hardly believe it...but I did and drove it! God is faithful when we believe Him for the impossible.

Do the Impossible

You can pray, "O God, do the impossible," and even say, "Lord, I am willing to pay the impossible." But, unless you're also willing to "go for it," you will never experience the impossible.

Hearts that dare to dream are encouraged by the fantastic story in I Samuel 17. Maybe you've read biblical accounts like this and said to yourself, "Now, that's great, but that can never happen to me." *Oh, yes it can!* David, as an Israelite teenager, was the only one in Israel who had enough faith in God to do the impossible: Stand up against eight-foot tall Goliath. The lad had only one weapon, a sling. And though he was accurate with it, his skill was all he had. Goliath had a helmet, a shield, and a huge sword. It was like going up against a grizzly bear armed with a peashooter. But David was confident. He believed God could do the impossible through him.

Meanwhile, the Philistine, with his shield bearer in front of him, kept coming closer to David. He looked David over and saw that he was only a boy. . .and he despised him. He said to David, "Am I a dog, that you come at me with sticks?" And the Philistine cursed David by his gods. "Come here," he said, "and I'll give your flesh to the birds of the air and the beasts of the field!"

David said to the Philistine, "You come against me with sword and spear and javelin, but I come against you in the name of the Lord Almighty, the God of the armies of Israel, whom you have defied. This day the Lord will hand you over to me, and I'll strike you down and cut off your head. Today I will give the carcasses of the Philistine army to the birds of the air and the beasts of the earth, and the whole world will know that there is a God in Israel (emphasis mine). *All those gathered here will know that it is not by sword or spear that the Lord saves; for the battle is the Lord's and he will give all of you into our hands."* (17:41-47)

Anybody can talk, but David was not only willing to

talk about doing the impossible, he also was willing to face the risks involved in doing it.

As the Philistine moved closer to attack him, David ran quickly toward the battle line to meet him. Reaching into his bag and taking out a stone, he slung it and struck the Philistine on the forehead. The stone sank into his forehead, and he fell face down on the ground.

(I Samuel 17:48-49)

There does come a time when all our words and positive thinking are not enough. Actively attempting the impossible is all that counts. Is your life on the line? Is your situation dark, filled with despair? Odds against you? You're in an impossible situation. It's now or never. You need a winning solution. What is it?

It's *God in you, doing the impossible—for Him!*

God accomplishes the impossible in our lives to bring glory to Him. Run your dreams through that test—then dare to believe in that impossible dream.

Always remember, as children of God and joint-heirs with the Lord Jesus Christ, winning is our heritage. If you feel like you're running on empty in the fast lane of life, look at your definition of success. Does it match God's? Or have you substituted something else as your standard? We are children of the King of Kings! Dare to be an *im*possibility believer.

As I was with Moses, so I will be with you; I will never leave you or forsake you. . .Be strong and very courageous. . . .Do not let this Book of the Law depart from your mouth; meditate on it day and night, so that you may be careful to do everything written in it. Then you will be prosperous and successful. Have I not commanded you? Be strong and courageous. Do not be terrified; do not be discouraged, for the Lord your God will be with you wherever you go. (Joshua 1:5-9)